# *The Missing Horse Mystery*

Nancy stopped and sniffed the air. Bess and Lee Anne stopped, too. "What's wrong?" Bess asked.

"Do you smell smoke?" Nancy asked.

Lee Anne lifted her chin and sniffed, too. "I smell something. We'd better find out where it's coming from. With all the hay and straw in here, this place would go up like a bonfire."

When Nancy moved down the aisle toward the other side of the barn, she noticed that the odor grew stronger.

Breaking into a jog, she took off for the other side. A curl of gray smoke wafted up from a stall to her right. A horse danced in front of the closed mesh door, its eyes wild with fright.

Nancy raced over to the stall. The horse whirled crazily, and now Nancy spotted flames leaping up from a pile of hay in the far corner.

"Fire!" Nancy screamed.

# Nancy Drew
# Mystery Stories

## Available from MINSTREL Books

# NANCY DREW® 145

## THE
## MISSING HORSE MYSTERY

## CAROLYN KEENE

A MINSTREL® BOOK

Published by POCKET BOOKS
New York   London   Toronto   Sydney   Tokyo   Singapore

A MINSTREL PAPERBACK *Original*

A Minstrel Book published by
POCKET BOOKS, a division of Simon & Schuster Inc.
1230 Avenue of the Americas, New York, NY 10020

Copyright © 1998 by Simon & Schuster Inc.
Produced by Mega-Books, Inc.

ISBN: 0-671-00754-8

First Minstrel Books printing October 1998

10  9  8  7  6  5  4  3  2

NANCY DREW, NANCY DREW MYSTERY STORIES, A MINSTREL BOOK and colophon are registered trademarks of Simon & Schuster Inc.

Cover art by Ernie Norcia

Printed in the U.S.A.

# Contents

# THE
# MISSING HORSE MYSTERY

# 1

## A Hot Beginning

"Look at that gorgeous horse!" Bess Marvin exclaimed as she looked out the passenger-side window of Nancy Drew's Mustang.

Nancy slowed the car and glanced at the horse being led along the grassy edge of the gravel drive. It was a sleek chestnut with rippling muscles.

As they drove past, the horse pranced sideways. "It *is* gorgeous," Nancy said. "I'll bet we see a lot of beautiful horses this weekend."

Nancy and Bess were at the Illinois Horse Park to attend the week-long Midwest Grand Prix Dressage Championships. They were meeting Bess's friend Lee Anne Suna. It was Friday morning, and Nancy and Bess were going to bunk with Lee Anne for a long weekend.

For the past year Lee Anne had been working for and training with former Olympic rider Klaus Schaudt at High Hills Farm. Nancy and Bess had had lunch with Lee Anne a week earlier, and she'd spent the entire time talking about the equestrian sport of dressage. Intrigued, Nancy and Bess had decided to attend the competition, and Lee Anne had insisted they stay at the motel with her.

Ned Nickerson, Nancy's boyfriend, was also meeting them at the show. His plan was to spend time with Nancy and Bess before his college semester got too busy.

"Too bad George couldn't come," Nancy commented.

"I'll bet she's having a great time teaching at the soccer clinic," Bess said as she scanned the showgrounds. She pointed to a large gray building. "There's Barn C. That's where Lee Anne said she'd meet us. All of the horses from High Hills Farm are there."

"It's good she told you exactly where we should meet her," Nancy said. "I had no idea the horse park was so big."

"And crowded," Bess added as a huge van rumbled by, enveloping the Mustang in a cloud of dust.

The parking lot was filled with horse trailers,

vans, and pickup trucks. Nancy drove around for a few minutes before she found a spot.

After she climbed out of the car, she shaded her eyes from the hot September sun and surveyed the grounds. From the lot, she could see the indoor arena, a cross-country jumping course, and a few barns, which seemed to Nancy to be the size of warehouses.

"The riding rings must be on the other side of the barns," Nancy said.

Bess gave Nancy a teasing look. "In dressage you ride in an arena," she said with a laugh.

"Well, *excuse me* for being so dense," Nancy shot back, then both girls burst out laughing.

Nancy reached inside the car and pulled out her baseball cap. She put it on over her reddish blond hair, pulling it down low to shade her face from the sun. Then she locked the car and joined Bess.

"How many horses did High Hills bring for the competition?" Nancy asked as they headed for Barn C. Both girls were prepared for the warm weather, wearing shorts, sneakers, and sunglasses. They'd also packed jeans and sweatshirts for the cooler evenings.

"I'm not sure. But the farm must share the barn with other competitors. The building looks big enough to hold fifty horses."

"At least," Nancy said after they stepped through the double doors. Before them stretched a long aisle with a concrete floor. Nancy guessed there were about fifty stalls on either side of the aisle—a hundred in all.

As Nancy walked down the aisle, she peered into the stalls. From each one a handsome horse looked back at her. Some were draped with coolers or fly sheets—lightweight covers to keep the flies off. Others had wraps only on their legs.

The stalls were spotless and thickly bedded with straw. Ceiling fans whirled overhead.

"Wow," Bess said. "This is like a fancy hotel. I wonder if this place has room service."

"Bess! Nancy!" a voice called.

Nancy looked over her shoulder and saw Lee Anne jogging down the aisle.

"Hey, you two," Lee Anne said. "I'm so glad you made it."

Bess's friend was small and slender. She wore cutoff jeans, a T-shirt that said "Dressage is my life," and paddock boots. Her brown hair was pulled back in a ponytail. Since she wasn't wearing makeup, Nancy thought she looked about twelve years old instead of nineteen.

"Lee Anne!" Bess gave her friend a hug. "We thought we'd never find you in this palace."

Lee Anne giggled. "Wait until you see *our* side of the barn. We really fixed it up."

"You mean there's another side?" Nancy asked.

4

"Amazing, isn't it?" Lee Anne said. "Barn C holds two hundred horses. There are over six hundred horses competing this week."

Lee Anne grabbed Bess's hand. "Come on." She began to tug her friend up the aisle. "I want you to see Aristocrat, Zanzibar, and Curio. Then I want you to meet Klaus and— "

"Michael?" Bess teased.

At lunch the week before, Lee Anne had talked a lot about a rider named Michael Raines, who was competing in the Grand Prix. From the way she'd described him, Nancy thought he sounded like a combination movie star, prince, and sports pro. Nancy and Bess couldn't wait to meet him.

Lee Anne blushed at Bess's teasing. "Of course you'll meet Michael. He's getting ready for a test, so you're just in time."

"Test?" Bess grinned. "Like multiple choice?"

"No, silly. His riding test. Dressage is a sport where the rider and horse perform a test made up of movements and figures. Michael's riding Intermediate Two tests. That's really advanced, but this fall he hopes to be riding Grand Prix, which is the highest level."

"Dressage seems pretty complicated," Bess said. "I hope I'll be able to follow what's going on."

"Don't worry. You'll understand after you've

been here for just a day." Lee Anne glanced at her watch. "We'd better hustle. Michael's on in forty-five minutes."

Lee Anne set a pace that made and Nancy and Bess jog to keep up. Halfway down the aisle, they turned right into a cross aisle that led to the other side of the stable.

When they rounded the corner, Lee Anne said, "There's Michael with Curio."

A young man stood beside a horse at the end of the aisle. The horse was a glossy bay. Its mane was braided and its hooves polished. It was bridled, and a lightweight blanket covered it from head to tail.

The man was elegantly dressed in a double-breasted black coat with long tails, a black top hat, and white breeches. High black boots reached to his knees.

"He looks as if he's going to a wedding," Bess joked in a low voice.

"That's called a shadbelly coat," Lee Anne said as she rushed up to Michael.

When he saw Lee Anne, Michael frowned impatiently. "Where were you? We've got to hurry. Curio needs a long time to warm up."

"I went to meet Nancy and Bess," Lee Anne explained. "You remember—the friends I told you about?"

"Nice meeting you." Michael gave them a

polite glance before turning his attention back to Lee Anne. "Meet me in the warm-up arena in fifteen minutes. And don't forget the fly spray."

Clucking to his horse, he left the barn, his boots echoing on the concrete floor.

Lee Anne flashed her friends an apologetic smile. "Sorry. He's really tense. This is his first time competing Curio, and his ride on Thursday in the warm-up class was just okay."

"Where's his regular horse?" Nancy asked.

"Midnight Blue's owner decided to show him herself."

"So Michael doesn't have a horse of his own?" Bess asked.

Lee Anne shook her head as she bent to put a jar of hoof polish into the grooming box. "Many dressage riders don't have horses of their own. Horses competing at Intermediate and Grand Prix levels cost a lot of money, so riders like Michael are at the mercy of the owners. He was ready to compete Midnight Blue this summer when his owner moved the horse to another stable."

"That doesn't seem fair," Bess said.

"It isn't. Curio's a fine horse, but still, Michael's had to start all over," she said gloomily. "He's trying to rack up enough good scores to qualify for the Pan American team. But now I don't know."

She pulled a spray bottle from the grooming box. "We've just got time to see Aristocrat before I have to meet Michael."

"That's Klaus Schaudt's horse, right?" Nancy remembered Lee Anne talking about the stallion at lunch.

Lee Anne's face brightened. "Right. Klaus has been competing him in Grand Prix since last year. They've done well, too, scoring in the sixty-five to seventy percentile range. They were even on the cover of my favorite horse magazine."

"So we're meeting a celebrity?" Bess said.

"Kind of," Lee Anne said. "Lots of dressage fans have come by to see Aristocrat up close and to get Klaus's autograph. Gilly's been busy."

"Gilly?" Nancy asked.

"Aristocrat's groom." Lee Anne walked over to a stall. "She even sleeps next to the horse."

The door to the stall was open, and Nancy glanced inside. A cot stood in one corner, a sleeping bag, duffel bag, and pillow neatly laid on top. Bales of hay filled up the other half of the stall.

"Gilly must be with Klaus," Lee Anne said. But here's Aristocrat."

Nancy joined Bess and Lee Anne in front of a steel-mesh door. In the stall, a brown horse was eating hay. When Lee Anne made a clucking noise, he turned his head to stare calmly at the trio. His coat gleamed, and his mane and tail were neatly brushed. Nancy was surprised that the celebrated horse looked like all the other brown horses in the barn.

"He looks like a horse even *I* could ride," Bess said, echoing Nancy's thoughts.

Lee Anne chuckled. "In Aristocrat's case, looks are deceiving. When Klaus rides him into an arena, it's as if a spotlight hits him. He might *look* like an ordinary horse, but he's worth about two hundred thousand dollars."

"Wow," Nancy said. "That *is* a lot of money." She looked closer, trying to imagine the horse leaping and prancing. Aristocrat only snorted.

Bess wrinkled her nose. "I guess we'll have to take your word for it."

"You don't need to take my word for it. Tomorrow you can watch him perform."

Anxiously, Lee Anne checked her watch. "Well, I'd better go help Michael. You guys should come and see his test. It'll be awesome, and I can explain what's happening."

"Sounds great," Nancy said as they headed up the aisle. "I'm really curious about dressage."

"Nan and I have been riding since we were about eight," Bess told her friend. "But we don't know very much about dressage."

As the three girls neared the cross aisle, Nancy stopped and sniffed the air.

Bess and Lee Anne stopped, too. "What's wrong?" Bess asked.

"Do you smell smoke?" Nancy asked.

There were No Smoking signs posted everywhere. Still, some careless person could have dropped a match or sneaked a cigarette in a stall, Nancy thought.

Lee Anne lifted her chin and sniffed, too. "I smell something. We'd better find out where it's coming from. With all the hay and straw in here, this place would go up like a bonfire."

Nancy turned in a circle, trying to figure out where the smell was coming from. When she moved down the aisle toward the other side of the barn, she noticed that the odor grew stronger.

Breaking into a jog, she took off for the other side. A curl of gray smoke wafted up from a stall to her right. A horse danced in front of the closed mesh door, its eyes wild with fright.

Nancy raced over to the stall. The horse whirled crazily, but Nancy spotted flames leaping up from a pile of hay in the far corner.

"Fire!" Nancy screamed.

# 2

# *A Clue*

Flipping the latch, Nancy threw open the stall door. The horse charged out, flattening Nancy against the outside wall, and bolted down the aisle.

Nancy ran into the stall. In the corner she could see that a pile of hay was burning. Lee Anne raced up, carrying an extinguisher. "Bess went to get Security," she gasped.

She aimed the nozzle of the fire extinguisher at the flames and pressed the lever. Foam spewed onto the fire. Nancy stomped on the edges of the flames to put out the embers.

"What are you doing in here?" a voice demanded. Nancy glanced over her shoulder. A woman wearing riding breeches stood in the doorway. Her face expressed her horror. "Where's my horse?"

"He ran down the aisle," Nancy told her. "There was a fire and your horse was frantic. When I opened the door, I couldn't stop him from running."

The woman ran in the direction Nancy pointed. Turning off the extinguisher, Lee Anne let out her breath. "Thank goodness you smelled the smoke, Nancy."

"What's going on in here?" a deep voice boomed. A huge man wearing a cowboy hat strode into the stall with Bess close behind him. He wore a tan uniform with a gold badge that read Chief of Security. Nancy could see the name R. Texel written on a name tag above the badge.

"There was a fire," Lee Anne explained. "But it's out now."

"A fire?" Texel tipped his hat back and scowled at the girls. "How'd it start? Were you girls smoking in here?"

"No, sir," Nancy said.

"Humph." He knelt down by the burned pile, his knees cracking. Eyes narrowed, he studied what was left of the hay.

Lee Anne nervously checked her watch. "Hey, everyone, I've got to run and help Michael. His test is in half an hour. You and Bess meet me at Arena One on top of the hill, okay?"

"As soon as we can," Nancy said. "I want to find out more about this fire."

Nancy was as curious about the fire as R. Texel. Her first hunch—that someone had dropped a match or a cigarette—didn't make sense. Would anyone do something so foolish? she wondered.

Texel pointed to the ashes. "Hay doesn't just catch on fire by itself. Let's see if anybody knows what happened." He turned and marched out of the stall.

"What do you think happened, Nancy?" Bess asked.

"I don't know. Let's look around and see if we can find anything." Nancy crouched down and poked through ashes. Finding nothing unusual in the blackened hay, she began to sift through the sawdust that had been used as bedding on this stall floor. Her fingers felt something long and flat.

"Look what I found." Nancy held up an unlit match torn from a matchbook. The head had several white streaks on it. "I wonder if the person who did this struck this match first. When it didn't light, he or she dropped it."

Nancy stood up and spoke, "Either someone was really careless—or this fire was set on purpose."

The two girls walked out into the aisle. The woman wearing the riding breeches was leading

13

her horse toward them. The horse's neck was dark with sweat. As it walked, Nancy noticed that it limped slightly on one of its front legs.

"Is your horse all right?" Nancy asked with concern.

The woman shook her head. "No. Secret bruised the sole of his hoof."

"Tough break," Bess said.

The woman smoothed the horse's forelock, tears filling her eyes. "Secret and I have been training all summer for this show. We're lucky it's just a bruise and not something worse."

Turning to Nancy and Bess, she held out her hand. "I'm Valerie Dunn. I want to thank you. Mr. Texel explained that your quick thinking saved Secret's life and possibly the lives of all the horses in the barn." She shuddered. "I can't imagine what would have happened if this place had caught fire."

"Ms. Dunn, do you have any idea how the hay—" Nancy started to ask.

"Just a second there, young lady." R. Texel strode up with a guard who was half his size. The name on his badge was A. Brackett.

Texel hooked his thumbs in his belt. "I'll ask the questions, if you don't mind."

"I don't mind," Nancy said with as much politeness as she could summon. She held out the match. "You might be interested in this. I found it in the sawdust." She dropped it into Texel's hand.

His bushy eyebrows rose, but he didn't say a word. Nancy and Bess said goodbye to Valerie Dunn, then headed toward the other end of the barn.

"Well," Bess said, "Mr. Texel made it clear he didn't want our help."

"Fine with me," Nancy said as they left through the same doors they'd entered earlier. "I want to have fun at the show, not hunt for an arsonist. Besides, Ned should be arriving any minute."

Stopping outside, Nancy scanned the parking lot. A tall, attractive young man with brown hair and an athletic build was striding toward them.

Nancy waved. "Ned!" she called.

"Hi, you two," he said as he jogged up. "How's the competition?"

"We've been too busy putting out a fire to see any of it yet," Bess replied.

"What happened?" Ned asked with concern.

"Someone dropped a match onto some hay," Nancy said. She guided him in the direction of the showgrounds. "We'll fill you in while we go to meet Lee Anne."

The trio made their way to the showgrounds. The area was crowded with horses of all sizes, colors, and shapes. Some were saddled and carried riders. Others were being walked, washed, or groomed. In one of the rings, several equestrians rode their mounts in small circles.

"There's Arena One." Nancy pointed to a flat rectangular area bordered by a low white fence. Twelve black letters on white boards were posted around the arena. "And there's Lee Anne."

Lee Anne was striding toward them, her arms filled with towels, jars, and sprays, which she dumped in a bucket under a tree. Nancy was about to introduce Ned when Lee Anne waved toward the arena. "Michael's just going in! If we hurry, we can watch from the hillside."

As they climbed the grassy slope, Lee Anne said, "I felt bad about leaving you, but Michael gets upset if I don't help him. There he is now."

Nancy sat beside Ned and Bess just as Michael and Curio trotted down the center of the arena. The pair halted in the middle. Picking up the rein in his left hand, Michael dropped his right hand and nodded to several people sitting at a table under a canopy.

"He's saluting the judge," Lee Anne whispered.

Ned leaned closer to Lee Anne. "What do all the letters around the arena mean?"

"The letters let the rider know where to execute each movement. For example, Michael knows he must halt and salute at the letter X, which is the center of the arena. Now he's tracking right at *C* and executing a circle at *R* . . ."

Ned and Bess stared at Lee Anne in confusion.

"Just watch," Lee Anne said with a grin.

Nancy tried to concentrate on the horse and rider, but her thoughts kept drifting back to the fire. Who had set it? she wondered. And why?

"Nancy." Lee Anne nudged her. "See the man under the big oak tree? That's Klaus Schaudt, Aristocrat's owner."

Nancy glanced at the man, noting his steel gray hair and military posture. A delighted gasp from Lee Anne drew her attention back to the arena. Michael and Curio were charging past, the horse's front legs reaching out.

"Did you see Curio's extended trot?" Lee Anne exclaimed. "Perfect!"

As the horse and rider rounded the corner, Nancy could see a look of intense concentration on Michael's face. At the letter *V*, Curio broke into a smooth, rocking canter, then cantered diagonally across the arena. Nancy thought Curio looked as if he were dancing.

"Next is the piroutte," Lee Anne said. She held her breath as horse and rider executed the move. "Perfect," Lee Anne murmured as Curio spun in a neat circle.

"That was beautiful," Nancy said. She watched as Curio trotted in place, lifting his legs high as if prancing to music. "I've never seen a horse perform such difficult movements."

"That's called the passage," Lee Anne explained.

"Wow." Bess whistled. "Getting a horse to dance must be tricky, but Michael makes it look easy."

"That's how it's supposed to seem. The horse should look as if he's performing on his own, but believe me, Michael's working hard."

Five minutes later Curio halted in the center again. When Michael saluted the judge, Lee Anne jumped to her feet and cheered loudly.

"Let's go congratulate him," she said. Picking up her bucket, she took off toward the arena exit.

Ned, Nancy, and Bess walked down the hill. Michael and Curio had stopped under the tree. Lee Anne held Curio's reins. Michael had dismounted and was loosening the horse's girth. Klaus Schaudt stood between Lee Anne and Michael.

As Nancy approached, she could see that Curio was breathing hard, his nostrils blowing in and out. Taking off his top hat, Michael handed it to Lee Anne. His hair was matted with sweat, and his mouth was pinched in an angry line.

No wonder, Nancy thought as she drew closer. Schaudt was admonishing him sternly. "Your flying changes were rough, Michael. The passage was only passable. Your scores will never get out

18

of the low sixties if you don't work on those two movements."

Nancy stopped a few feet away, Ned and Bess behind her. Michael's face was bright red. Lee Anne stared down at the reins in her hand.

"We didn't get enough time to practice the test during warm up," Michael said through clenched teeth.

The man frowned at Lee Anne. "And why not? You were supposed to coach him."

"I—I'm sorry," Lee Anne stammered. "There was a fire in one of the stalls and—"

"A fire?" Michael whirled to face her.

"Whose stall?" Schaudt demanded. "One of our horses?"

"No," Nancy said quickly, stepping toward the trio. "I'm Nancy Drew, Lee Anne's friend." Taking Schaudt's hand, she shook it firmly, then introduced Ned and Bess. "The horse belonged to a woman named Valerie Dunn. When it bolted from the stall, it bruised the sole of its hoof."

Michael snorted with amusement. "Too bad for Valerie, though I'm sure glad she won't be able to compete against me."

Nancy was surprised by his unsportsmanlike comment. Did he really mean it or was he just reacting to the pressure?

"Ha!" Schaudt scoffed. "If you don't improve your performance, Valerie could beat you with a *lame* horse."

19

Turning his attention to Nancy, Ned, and Bess, Schaudt smiled so warmly that Nancy found it hard to believe he was the same person who had just chewed Michael out. "It's nice to meet you and your friends, Miss Drew. Now if you'll excuse me . . ."

With a nod of his head, he strode off across the showgrounds. Michael scowled, then jerked the reins from Lee Anne's hand and led Curio away.

Lee Anne blew out her breath. "Sorry you had to hear that. Klaus is very demanding, and he's been especially hard on Michael these past few days." She flashed them an apologetic grin. "Which means Michael's under tons of pressure. He hasn't been himself lately."

"I know how intense sports competitions can get," Ned said.

"Well, I'd better help Michael cool Curio off," Lee Anne said. Tucking the top hat under her arm, she bent to pick up the bucket. "Why don't you stay and watch some of the other horses?" she added before hurrying off.

"Whew," Bess said when Lee Anne had gone. "I sure wouldn't want to work with Klaus Schaudt, no matter how wonderful a trainer he is. And I don't care what excuses Lee Anne makes—I think Michael's rude."

"Give the guy a break," Ned said. "He might be totally different when he's not stressed."

Nancy reluctantly agreed. "Lee Anne did say

he was trying to earn high scores at this show so he could qualify for—"

Loud yelling cut Nancy off.

Behind Bess, a young man was struggling to hold on to a horse that was shaking its head so wildly it jerked the lead line from the man's grasp.

Nancy gasped as the horse wheeled and raced in their direction. Eyes wild with fright, it slid to a stop right behind Bess. As it reared, Nancy could see that its hooves were inches from Bess's head.

# 3

## Thief!

"Bess!" Nancy screamed. Grabbing her friend's wrist, she yanked her out of the path of the horse's hooves. Bess crashed into Nancy, and the two of them landed in a heap on the ground. The horse loomed over them, its nostrils flaring.

"Whoa." Speaking calmly, Ned stepped toward the animal and caught the dangling lead line. Bess scrambled to her feet, pulling Nancy with her. At the same time the young man ran around and took the lead from Ned.

The man backed the horse up, then stopped it. As he patted the horse's neck, he spoke in a soothing voice. Listening closely, she realized he was speaking German.

22

"Thanks, Nan," Bess said as she brushed off the seat of her shorts.

Stooping, Nancy picked up her cap, which had fallen off. "Thank Ned. He kept us from getting trampled."

"Are you all right?" The young man came up to them, a worried expression on his face. After pulling off his cap, he held it against his chest. In his other hand he held the lead tightly, but by now his horse was standing docilely by his side.

"Yes. We're fine," Nancy told him.

"Thank goodness." He blew out an exaggerated breath. "I would not want two beautiful American women to be stomped to death."

Bess giggled. The man grinned at her, his blue eyes twinkling. He had wavy blond hair, a slim, athletic rider's build, and an infectious smile.

"Gunter Werth." He took Bess's hand and shook it heartily. "And you two ladies are . . . ?"

"Bess Marvin." Bess shook his hand. "And these are my friends Nancy Drew and Ned Nickerson."

"I am honored to meet you." Gunter bowed at the waist, then straightened up. "Well, Bess, Nancy, and Ned, my horse, Persaldo, apologizes for his rude behavior." He grinned boyishly. "Perhaps you would accept my invitation to dinner tonight as an apology?"

Bess grinned. "That sounds wonderful, Gunter, but I . . . we hardly know you."

23

"And I hardly know anyone in this country," Gunter said wistfully. "I need someone to show me the sights and explain American words—like why they call it a hot *dog* and why everyone says 'awesome.'"

"Why don't *you* join *us?*" Ned suggested. "We'll answer your questions about America if you'll answer our questions about dressage. We're newcomers to the sport."

"Ah." Gunter smoothed his hair and put his cap back on. "Dressage is a tricky sport to understand, but it's beautiful to watch. I will be happy to—how do you say it?—fill you in."

They agreed to meet at the motel at seven-thirty. Reluctantly Bess said goodbye as Gunter led his horse away.

"Wow," she gasped. "He's really nice. Ned, thanks for inviting him to have dinner with us."

"We can ask Lee Anne and Michael, too," Nancy suggested. "Make it a fun night out."

Bess groaned. "A *fun* night with Michael? No way."

"Let's give the guy a chance," Nancy said. "Lee Anne seems to like him, so there must be something to like."

"I doubt it." Bess shook her head. "Now, with Gunter there's a lot to like. He knows how to charm a girl. Not like you American guys." She playfully punched Ned on the arm. "Always

24

taking us for granted and expecting us to fall all over you."

"Take *Nancy* for granted?" Ned joked. "Never. She might stick a scorpion in my bed."

"Don't give me ideas, Nickerson," Nancy teased back.

"Hey, speaking of ideas"—Bess pointed to a little girl eating a chili dog—"let's eat. In fact"—she pulled a brochure from the pocket of her shorts—"according to this, the concourse of the indoor arena is filled with over fifty vendors!"

"Oh, great." Ned rolled his eyes. "Shopping."

"Good idea," Nancy said. "After we find something to eat, we can browse. Then I'd like to stop by the security office to see if they found any clues about the fire."

The three of them headed for the huge arena. It was dark and cool inside, a welcome respite from the intense sun.

After Nancy's eyes adjusted, she looked around. Bess was right. The top level of the circular concourse was filled with vendors' booths. Most were hawking horse supplies, but others sold jewelry, handmade clothing, and leather goods.

Bess's eyes glowed as she made a beeline for a glass case filled with silver and turquoise earrings. "A pair of these would look great with my new blouse."

Ned strolled over to a rack of hand-tooled

leather belts while Nancy headed for a booth selling old books. She scanned the shelves, noticing that all the books were about horses. She found one of her childhood favorites. Pulling it out, she flipped through the pages, admiring the illustrations.

"That would be a neat present for Lee Anne," Bess said over her shoulder.

They browsed for a few more minutes, waiting for Ned. When he finally rejoined them, he wore a new belt in the loops of his denim shorts.

"What do you think?" he asked, putting his thumbs behind the silver buckle to show it off.

"I think for someone who hated the idea of shopping, you did really well," Nancy joked. "You look like a cowboy."

"Ready to eat?" Bess asked.

The three stood in line at a concession stand. After they'd received their orders, they sat at a small round table overlooking the indoor ring below. Rows and rows of seats sloped down to the circular area where several riders schooled their horses.

As Nancy munched her tuna salad on whole wheat, she watched the horses move effortlessly, with their necks arched and their heads tucked in, their legs rising and falling in perfect rhythm.

"Dressage is an art as well as a sport," she commented.

"Umm." Bess nodded in agreement as she ate a

french fry. Ned was polishing off his second chili dog.

"And by the time we leave on Sunday night, we should know all about it," Bess added after a sip of soda.

When they were finished eating, Bess decided to do some more shopping. "I think I'll get one of those children's books for Lee Anne. And maybe those earrings and a T-shirt and—" She broke off with a grin.

"Ned and I are going to stop by Security," Nancy said. "We'll meet you at Barn C."

After saying goodbye, Ned and Nancy hunted for the security office. It was located near the front entrance off the concourse. Peeking inside, Nancy saw two desks and three file cabinets.

Texel sat at the far desk. He was leaning back in a swivel chair, his boots propped up on the seat of a second chair. A phone receiver was wedged between his shoulder and his ear. While he talked into the phone, he ate a hamburger. Waving the last bite in the air, he gestured for Nancy and Ned to come in.

"I'll get back to ya," he said, then hung up. "What can I do for you?" he asked Nancy and Ned.

"We were wondering if you'd discovered anything more about the fire," Nancy said.

Texel crumpled the hamburger wrapper and tossed it into a trash can.

"And why are you so curious?" he asked. "Maybe because Chief McGinnis tells me you're some kind of teen detective."

"Chief McGinnis?" Nancy asked. "How did you know we were from River Heights? And how do you know the chief?"

"Hey, my job's finding things out." Texel grinned. "McGinnis and I go way back. I was a county deputy for twenty-five years, sheriff for the last five. This is my retirement job."

He stood and stretched. "No leads on the fire," he said. "We tried to question everyone who has horses in Barn C. No one heard or saw anything. Of course, I've only got three guys to watch over this place on each shift, and with one at the gate all day checking passes, that doesn't leave much manpower for tracking down clues."

"Do you think the fire was deliberately set?" Ned asked.

"No. I think it was just plain stupid," Texel said. "Somebody went into the stall and lit a cigarette and is probably too embarrassed to admit it."

"Probably." Nancy thought back to the dropped match. Was Texel right? She didn't think a sheriff with so much experience would miss much. Of course, if he did know something, he might not want to tell her.

"Thank you for the information." Linking her arm through Ned's, Nancy turned to leave.

"Ms. Drew." Texel's stern voice stopped her. "You let me in on anything you find out, you hear."

Nancy nodded, though she could tell by his tone that he wasn't asking a question. R. Texel was used to giving orders.

"He's a tough one," Ned commented as they left the office.

Nancy headed for the exit. "Let's hope he can figure out who started that fire. I'd hate to think an arsonist is loose at this show."

When they got outside, Nancy slowed down to put on her cap and sunglasses. "We need to meet Bess at Barn C. Let's walk through one of the other barns to get there. It will be cooler, and I love looking at the horses."

They hurried toward Barn A. When they stepped inside, they found the aisle deserted.

"Texel's right. There isn't much security for a place this size," Nancy said. "It's strange, considering how valuable the horses are."

"I guess the owners are supposed to keep track of their own horses," Ned said. He walked with Nancy over to a stall. A huge gray horse stared back at them. "Though it seems as if they're not doing a very good job," Ned added.

"I agree," Nancy said. "Anyone could just walk into these barns."

A scream echoed through the barn.

"What was that!" Ned cried.

Nancy held her breath.

"Stop him!" The cry came from the other side of the barn.

"Let's go!" Nancy grabbed Ned's hand and they took off down the aisle. At the intersection, they turned left. As they reached the other side of the barn, a woman came running toward them.

Her cheeks were flushed, and she pointed toward the far end of the barn. "Stop him!" she cried.

Nancy whirled in time to see a man dart out of the barn. All she could make out was the tan shirt he was wearing. Halfway down the aisle Nancy saw a horse with its lead line dangling from its halter.

"Stop him!" the woman shouted. "He was trying to steal my horse!"

# 4

## A Clean Getaway

Ned and Nancy ran down the aisle. When they passed the horse, it skittered sideways. The woman ran up and caught the lead before the horse could bolt.

Nancy raced outside. The sun was blindingly bright, and she stopped short. She looked toward the showgrounds. The area was swarming with horses, riders, and spectators. "There's no way we'll find him in that crowd," she told Ned in frustration.

"Maybe he went in the other direction," Ned said.

Glancing toward the parking lot, Nancy caught sight of a man disappearing behind a van. "That could be him!" she cried. "He's wearing a tan shirt, just like the person who ran from the barn. Let's split up."

With a nod, Ned circled left around the rows of cars. Nancy sprinted right, weaving her way past trailers and trucks. When she reached the van, she dashed to the other side. There was no sign of the fleeing man.

Ned jogged up. "I think we lost him."

"We did," Nancy said. "He could be anywhere. This parking lot's as big as a football field."

"Let's get help," Ned suggested. "Texel and his men should be alerted."

Nancy agreed. When they reached the barn, Texel was already there with two uniformed guards. They were talking to the woman who had discovered the thief. She'd phoned Security as soon as she'd caught her horse.

"Ms. Drew," Texel declared. "What are *you* doing here?"

Nancy waved toward the parking lot. "We heard someone yell for help. We saw a man flee and followed him to the parking lot."

"And you know for sure it was the thief?" Texel asked.

"No, but it was a man, and he was—"

"Ms. Drew there are hundreds of men here today," Texel cut her off.

Nancy fumed for a second, then added, "He

was wearing a tan shirt, just like the person in the aisle."

"Oh. Still"—Texel stuck a finger in Nancy's face—"you leave this to Security." Stepping away, he spoke into his walkie-talkie. Nancy couldn't hear his words, but she hoped he was alerting his men. When he turned back, he ignored Nancy and Ned. "Now, Ms. Flanagan, finish your story."

Nancy gritted her teeth. Part of her wanted to take Texel's advice and leave, but the detective part of her wanted to hear Ms. Flanagan's story.

"I was outside washing buckets when I heard the clunk of hooves on the concrete aisle," Ms. Flanagan began. She was dressed in baggy shorts and an oversize denim shirt. A bandanna covered her gray hair. "I thought it was odd because the people who have horses in this section of the barn were either at lunch, riding, or watching the competition. When I ducked around the doorway to see what was going on, I saw a man hurrying down the aisle—*with my horse!*"

"Did you recognize him?" Texel asked.

Ms. Flanagan shook her head. "He had his back to me, and for a second I was so stunned I just stood there. When I finally hollered, he turned. I caught a glimpse of his face and—" Hesitating, she plucked at her lip as if unsure of what to say. "Well, he looked . . . deformed or something," she finally said.

"You mean he had a scar?" Texel asked.

"No. More like he'd been burned all over his face." She touched both cheeks to show what she meant.

Nancy tried to picture the man she'd glimpsed in the parking lot. Had his face been disfigured? she wondered.

Texel rubbed his chin. "Now, Ms. Flanagan, someone who fit that description would stand out in a crowd. Are you sure that's what you saw?"

"I only saw him for a second," Ms. Flanagan said. "When I yelled again, he dropped the lead and ran. I was so worried about my horse, I didn't pay attention to him after that."

Texel looked at Nancy. "Does that sound like the man you saw in the parking lot?"

"I didn't see his face," Nancy reluctantly admitted.

Texel turned to his two men. "Circulate the description to the other guards. Then start interviewing everybody in this barn. I want to find that man. Rumors of a horse thief will stir this place up worse than hornets."

Nancy was turning to leave when Texel touched her arm. "I could use your help," he said in a low voice.

"What?" She was surprised by his request.

"There are as many as fifty horse owners in this barn alone," he said to her and Ned. "I can't pull all my guards off duty to interview everybody. I'd

34

appreciate you talking to anyone who rides or owns a horse in this barn. Somebody might know this guy."

"We'll be happy to help," Nancy said. Ned added his agreement.

"Good." Nodding curtly, Texel strode off. "And report to me as soon as you know anything," he called over his shoulder.

"Well, Nan, looks like you were recruited by the chief himself," Ned said.

"*We* were recruited." Nancy took his hand. "Do you mind?"

He grinned. "No. I love a good mystery as much as you do."

Nancy checked her watch. "We'd better meet Bess and tell her what's going on."

As they headed for Barn C, Nancy thought about the two incidents. The fire and the attempted theft had happened in different barns. Still, she wondered if there was a connection.

When they found Bess, she was showing Lee Anne and another girl her new earrings.

"Nancy and Ned," Bess said, "meet Gilly Phillips, Aristocrat's groom. She takes care of Klaus Schaudt's horse—day and night."

"Hi." The girl smiled shyly. Her short wavy hair was so blond it looked white. She was dressed in jeans, paddock boots, and a tank top. Her figure was trim, and her arms were tanned and muscular.

Nancy and Ned told the others about the would-be horse thief.

"I know Roberta Flanagan," Lee Anne said. "She owns several terrific horses. In fact, in the last show she and her horse Sweet and Klean won the Intermediate One competition."

"Blew Michael right out of the competition," Gilly said matter-of-factly.

Lee Anne rolled her eyes. "Don't remind me. He stewed for days."

"Well, I hope they catch the thief." Gilly glanced nervously into Aristocrat's stall. The brown horse pressed his nose against the mesh door and blew softly. "The grounds are full of valuable horses."

"Just how much is a horse like Aristocrat worth?" Nancy asked.

"I think Klaus has him insured for two hundred thousand dollars," Gilly said.

Ned whistled. "Wow. That's a lot of money."

"Yes, but he's a good investment. Aristocrat is passing on his talent to his foals. They're gorgeous, smart, and fantastic movers. Even when Aristocrat can't compete anymore, he'll still be valuable as a stallion."

"The chief of security has asked us to help him interview owners and riders in Barn A," Nancy said. "He's hoping someone noticed a man with a scarred face."

"I'll help you talk to people," Bess volunteered.

"Good." Nancy looked at Lee Anne and Gilly.

Lee Anne raised one hand, palm out. "Count me out. I have to school a horse, bathe Curio, then braid another horse."

"I won't be able to help, either." Gilly stooped to pick up a bucket of cleaning supplies. "If I leave Aristocrat for too long, Klaus bawls me out. Now I know why he's so edgy. It would be easy to steal a horse at a show."

"Why isn't security tighter?" Nancy asked.

"More security would be difficult," Lee Anne explained. "They check passes at the gate, and the grounds are fenced. Still, people drive in and out day and night with horses in trailers. Even if you have a full-time groom, your horse is left alone sometimes, which means anyone could open up a stall, lead your horse out, load him on a trailer, and leave. Horses don't wear dog tags, so it would be impossible for anyone to check the identity of every horse coming and going."

"Can't you lock the stall doors?" Bess asked.

Gilly shook her head. "Too dangerous if a fire breaks out."

Nancy thought about the new information. If the horses were even half as valuable as Aristocrat, a show like this would be the perfect target for thieves.

After the group said goodbye, Nancy, Ned, and Bess started back to Barn A. Nancy stopped halfway there. "Before we start talking to owners and riders, let's check the parking lot one more time."

"What do you think you're going to find?" Ned asked.

"I'm not sure. But if the man was intent on stealing the horse, he must have had a van or trailer, as Gilly said, to haul the horse away. Maybe someone saw a man with a scarred face leave. It would be great if we could get a car or truck license number."

"That only happens on TV shows," Bess said.

Nancy laughed. "Maybe we'll get lucky."

Bess and Ned went over to talk to a man unloading a horse while Nancy wandered toward the van where she'd seen the man disappear. She tried to follow what she thought might be the path he would have taken from the barn, just in case he'd dropped something.

When she reached the van, she checked it over carefully. Twin Meadows Stables was written on the side of the big truck, with a city and state written underneath. Nancy doubted a thief would drive off in something so conspicuous. Still, she tried the cab doors. They were both locked, and the ramp to the back was shut tightly.

When she went to the other side of the van, she noticed it was parked next to a gray horse trailer. The trailer had been unhitched from the vehicle that towed it, so it stood by itself. The back doors and ramp were secured, but when Nancy walked around to the far side, she noticed that the door leading to the front of the trailer was ajar.

She stopped. Maybe the open door simply meant the owner had been careless. Or maybe someone—like a fleeing thief—had used the trailer to hide inside.

Nancy knew she had to check it out. Glancing over her shoulder, she hunted for Bess or Ned. Neither was in sight.

Taking hold of the handle, she pulled the door open. The inside of the trailer was dark.

Stooping, she stuck her head inside. A net full of hay hung from a center post. She pushed it aside, and her heart leaped into her throat.

A man's face leered down at her, his lips distorted in a twisted smirk. One eye dangled from a bloody socket. The other was fixed on her in a hideous stare!

# 5

## *Suspicious*

Nancy recoiled from the grotesque face, banging her head on the top of the doorframe. With a scream, she flung herself away from the trailer.

Heart racing, she backed away, bumping into the van behind her. For a second she stood frozen in fear, her gaze riveted on the open door.

In a flash her mind replayed the image of the face—the slack skin, misshapen head, and dangling eye—and suddenly she realized what she had seen: a mask.

"Nancy!" Bess and Ned came running from the other side of the parking lot.

Ned reached her first. "Are you all right?" He

placed both hands on her shoulders, then gave her a hug.

Still shaken, Nancy could only nod. Ned looked toward the open door. "Is something in there?" His fingers tightened on her shoulders.

Bess jogged up, gasping for breath. Her eyes widened when she, too, saw the gaping doorway. "Who . . . what's in there?" she stammered.

Nancy shook her head. "It's all right. No one's in there. At least no one human."

Ned cocked one eyebrow at her. Nancy walked up to the trailer door, leaned in, and reached around the hay net. When her fingers touched the lifelike latex skin of the mask, she shivered.

After pulling out the mask, she held it over her face, then turned toward her friends. Bess shrieked.

"Meet our thief," Nancy said as she lowered the mask.

"You mean the guy wore a mask?" Ned asked.

Nancy stretched it out. The skin color and texture made it look real. "Right. No wonder Roberta Flanagan said he looked deformed."

Bess wrinkled her nose. "That thing is really creepy-looking."

"But effective," Nancy said. "Our thief is being careful not to be identified."

Ned touched the bulging eye. "We'd better show this to Texel."

"We should bring Texel here," Nancy said. "I'm going to hang the mask back up in the trailer so he can see where it was. He and his men might find fingerprints inside the trailer, too."

Bess pointed to the side of the trailer. "Look, there's a dent right over the wheel. That will help us remember which one it is."

After climbing inside the trailer, Nancy hung the mask back on the hook. Pushing aside the hay net, she peered over the divider into the back of the trailer. Was the thief planning to use this to haul away a stolen horse?

The trailer wasn't hitched to a vehicle, but Nancy thought maybe the thief was going to back a truck up to it later, after the excitement had died down.

Nancy could only hope that they'd catch the thief before he did steal a horse.

Ned led the way back to Barn A, where they found Texel talking to a half dozen irate horse owners. One of the owners was shouting about the lack of security.

"We're doing everything we can," Texel explained.

The owner didn't act reassured. "If someone almost got away with stealing a horse, it's not enough."

Gesturing for Nancy, Ned, and Bess to follow him, Texel moved down the aisle and away from the crowd. Nancy figured he was grateful for an excuse to get away.

"Did you find anything?" he asked, his tone urgent.

"We found a mask in one of the trailers," Nancy told him.

"A mask, huh?" Rocking back on the heels of his boots, Texel gave Nancy, Bess, and Ned a skeptical look.

"We *all* saw it," Bess said emphatically.

"And it explains why Ms. Flanagan thought the thief's face was deformed," Nancy added.

"All right," Texel said. "Let's go look at it."

Nancy led the way through the parked vehicles with Ned, Bess, and Texel right behind her. When she rounded the Twin Meadows van, she stopped dead.

The gray horse trailer was gone.

"Hey, where'd it go?" Bess asked in surprise. "Wasn't this where it was parked?"

Ned looked around. "Yes. Someone must have moved it."

"All right, where's this mask?" Texel asked. His face was red from the hike in the hot sun. Sweat rolled down his forehead.

"Uh . . ." Nancy glanced at Ned, but he could only shrug his shoulders. "It was in the trailer that *used* to be parked right here."

"You mean you lost a trailer?" Texel scowled.

Ned, Nancy, and Bess all nodded.

"Wait a minute. Is this some kind of prank?" Texel's voice grew low and threatening. "Some kind of early Halloween joke?"

"No, sir," Nancy said quickly. "I know it seems strange, but somebody must have seen me find the mask. As soon as we left, he or she moved the trailer."

"Look, there are some marks in the gravel." Ned pointed to what could have been a tire track. "It took us about fifteen minutes to find you and get back here. That gave somebody plenty of time to hitch up the trailer and take it somewhere else."

Texel wiped his brow with a handkerchief. "That's a lot of if's." After folding the handkerchief, he stuffed it back in his pocket. "Next time be sure you've got something." With an exasperated grunt at Nancy, Bess, and Ned, Texel stomped off.

Ned threw up his hands. "That's it. I'm not helping Texel anymore. He and his men can solve their own crimes."

"I agree," Bess said.

"He's just frustrated because he's not getting anywhere and everybody's breathing down his neck," Nancy said. Hands on hips, she scanned the parking lot. "So do you think the trailer's still on the showgrounds?"

Bess and Ned groaned.

"Nancy!" Bess declared. "Give it up. Didn't you hear Texel?"

"Yeah, yeah." Nancy grinned at her two friends. Bess's nose was getting sunburned, and Ned's brow was sweaty. "Let's get something to drink, then see what Lee Anne's up to. I feel as if we've spent our whole day hunting for nonexistent criminals."

"That's because we have," Ned said as they started back.

As Nancy followed her friends, she thought about the attempted theft, the mask, and the disappearing trailer. All the clues added up to one thing—the thief was someone who knew the showgrounds and could slip in and out of the barns without raising anyone's suspicion. Someone who had to wear a mask so he wouldn't be recognized.

But who?

Nancy let out a breath in frustration. Hundreds of men at the show fit that description—owners, grooms, riders. Texel and his guards couldn't watch every horse every second.

When the trio reached Barn C, they found Lee Anne in the aisle grooming a horse in cross ties.

"You found a mask?" She looked as surprised as Texel after they had told her the story.

"And lost it again," Bess said.

Lee Anne giggled. "Wearing a mask sounds like something Michael would do. Last October

45

he scared Gilly and me half to death with a Halloween mask. He popped out of one of the stalls."

Nancy patted the horse. The name Divine was etched on a brass nameplate on the side of his halter. "What did the mask look like?"

"Kind of like this." Twisting her lips, Lee Anne grimaced at Nancy. "Only worse because one of the eyeballs hung out."

Nancy's eyebrows shot up; Ned's jaw dropped; and Bess reacted by opening her eyes wide in surprise.

"What?" Lee Anne stopped brushing the horse. "What did I say?"

"Nothing!" Nancy blurted out. She shot Ned and Bess a don't-say-a-word warning.

Instantly Bess plucked a curry comb from the grooming box. "Need help?" she asked.

"Sure." Lee Anne gestured to the horse's other side. "I need to get Divine polished and ready for this evening. Michael's riding him in an Intermediate One test."

Nancy was glad Bess had distracted Lee Anne. There was no way Nancy wanted her to know that she had just described the mask the thief had worn.

"Ned, didn't you want to look at those belts again?" Nancy asked him. Taking Ned's hand, she tugged him down the aisle.

"Uh, sure," Ned said. "We'll see you guys later," he called.

When they were out of earshot, Nancy stopped outside the barn door. "Did you hear that? Lee Anne described the mask perfectly!" she exclaimed.

"Do you think Michael's involved?" Ned asked.

"I don't know. We'll have to find out where he was after he rode. Still, the facts do add up." Nancy put up a finger. "Number one, he knows the barns. Two, he knows the horse that was almost stolen. Three, he needs money. Four, he had a mask like the thief's."

"I don't know, Nan. Lee Anne keeps saying how ambitious Michael is. Why would a rider working toward being on the Pan American team jeopardize his chances by stealing a horse?"

Nancy's eyes lit up. "Maybe because the theft might actually improve his chances! Come on. I need to check out a hunch."

Nancy hurried across the showgrounds to the secretary's booth, a place where owners and riders entered their horses, paid fees, and checked on their standings. The small building was bustling with activity.

"May I see the entry list for this evening's Intermediate One test?" Nancy asked a harried woman who was pulling prize ribbons from a box.

Without pausing, the woman nodded to a stack of papers. "It would be in there."

Leafing through the stack of papers, Nancy found the list. All the horses and riders entered in the test Michael was riding that evening were itemized.

Nancy ran her finger down the list. There. Roberta Flanagan and Sweet and Klean.

"Look," she whispered excitedly to Ned. "Roberta and her horse are competing against Michael and Curio tonight. Gilly said that at the last show, Sweet and Klean beat Michael by a lot. That gives Michael another reason to steal her horse—he's so competitive, he'd do *anything* to win."

# 6

## *Missing!*

"Stealing a horse just to win a class at a horse show?" Ned shook his head in disbelief. "That seems pretty far-fetched, Nan."

"Not if you're as competitive as Michael." Nancy continued to flip through the prize lists. "Don't you remember what he said when he heard that Valerie Dunn's horse had injured its hoof? Michael seemed positively happy."

Ned shrugged. "That just proves he likes to win."

"This is what I was hunting for." Nancy held up a list of riders entered in an Intermediate Two test scheduled for the next morning. "Look." She tapped her finger on a name halfway down the list. "Valerie Dunn. She was supposed to compete against Michael tomorrow."

"That does seem like more than a coincidence," Ned agreed.

As Nancy stacked the prize lists, she mulled over the evidence that pointed to Michael. He'd been warming up Curio when the fire was set, so he couldn't have been responsible for that incident. Unless he was working with someone. But who? And what would that person's motive be?

She shook her head, realizing how few answers she had. "At dinner tonight we need to keep our ears and eyes open," Nancy told Ned as they left the secretary's booth. "Michael may let something important slip."

Ned made a face. "Hey, what happened to having a plain old fun evening?"

Smiling up at him, Nancy linked her arm through his. "Oh, I think we can manage to fit in a little fun."


"So, what do you think, Bess?" Nancy turned slowly, modeling her new skirt and red top. Her hair was brushed back in soft waves, and her cheeks were tanned from the day in the sun.

"You look great." Bess wore a knit dress and sandals. Her new turquoise earrings dangled from her ears.

It was seven o'clock. The two girls were dressing in the room they were sharing with Lee Anne. They were about to meet Ned and Gunter.

"You look great, too," Nancy said as she swung open the door to the room. "We'd better hurry. Lee Anne and Michael are picking us up out front."

"Michael's driving?" Bess asked as they walked into the hall.

"Right. He borrowed one of Klaus's cars." Nancy locked the door, then followed Bess down the corridor. When they reached the lobby, the girls spied Ned and Gunter.

Gunter was wearing new jeans and a light blue shirt with a button-down collar. His sleeves were rolled up casually, and his wavy blond hair was slicked down. Ned was dressed in khakis and a polo shirt.

"Hey, you two look great," Ned said.

"You don't look too shabby either," Bess answered.

Gunter pointed proudly to the label on his jeans. "This brand is hard to get in Germany. I bought five pairs to take home."

"How long will you be in Illinois?" Bess asked as they headed for the main doors.

"About a month. Usually Americans come to Germany to train in dressage," he explained. "But I wanted to learn more about American techniques."

As they stepped outside, Michael and Lee Anne were just pulling up.

"Our chariot awaits," Ned whispered to Nancy as they approached a dusty, dented station wagon. Ned opened the back door, then gestured for Nancy to climb in. Nancy slid in next to Bess, who'd gotten in from the other side.

Lifting her nose, she sniffed. The whole car smelled like manure. She glanced over her shoulder. The back of the wagon was piled high with buckets, blankets, and a bag of grain.

"Ah, what a great aroma," Gunter said.

"It must be Nancy's new perfume," Ned joked, and everybody laughed.

Michael drove the car out of the motel drive. While the others talked about the show, he stared intently ahead, as if preoccupied. Nancy wondered what he was thinking.

"I invited Gilly along," Lee Anne said, "but after that horse was almost stolen, Klaus was adamant about her keeping an eye on Aristocrat all night."

"That doesn't sound like much fun," Bess said.

Michael snorted. "She's not paid to have fun."

Lee Anne frowned at him. Since Lee Anne was sharing the room with Nancy and Bess, Nancy knew how much time and effort she had taken with her makeup and hair. Nancy bet Michael hadn't even noticed how pretty Lee Anne looked.

"Where are we going to eat?" Ned asked.

"I thought we'd try the Steak House," Lee Anne said. "Klaus recommended it, and it's just a five-minute drive away."

Fifteen minutes later the group was seated around a large table overlooking a pasture filled with horses. A round of sodas had been served.

Lee Anne and Gunter were explaining the different dressage movements to Bess, Nancy, and Ned. Michael had slumped down in his seat, his expression sullen.

Michael was handsome, Nancy decided after watching him for a moment. She knew a lot of girls would be attracted to him. Still, she wondered why Lee Anne seemed so crazy about him. Even away from the showgrounds, he acted tense. Except for their interest in horses, they seemed to have nothing in common.

"The Grand Prix is the ultimate test." Nancy tuned in to what Lee Anne was saying. "The horse has to perform difficult movements like the passage you saw Curio do this morning during his test."

Michael rolled his eyes. "You'd hardly call that hopping up and down a passage."

Lee Anne cleared her throat. "Well, I thought you did fine—"

"Except it's what the judges thought that counts," Michael cut her off. "And they showed me what they thought by giving me a score of sixty-four."

"Sixty-four's pretty good," Gunter said.

Michael turned his dark eyes on him. "Right. Like you'd be satisfied with a sixty-four."

"If my horse did his best, yes." Gunter nodded emphatically.

"That's a laugh. You Germans never score lower than a sixty-seven. So even if my horse did his best, you'd still win. Just like in the Olympics."

Slowly Gunter set down his soda glass. "Would you like to explain that remark?" he asked politely.

"You know what I'm talking about. Dressage is big business in your country. You have sponsors who pay for everything. You don't have to worry about whether or not you'll have a horse to ride or how you're going to pay for everything."

"You have good horses here."

"Your castoffs. Curio would be a mediocre horse in Germany."

"Michael!" Lee Anne protested. "That's not true. Why don't you quit arguing and just have a good time?"

Throwing down his napkin, Michael stood up abruptly. "I'd love to, but I've got more important things to do. Like proving to the judges that I'm as good as the European riders. Good night and enjoy your dinner," he said. Turning, he stormed out of the restaurant.

"What was that all about?" Bess asked.

Gunter shook his head. "*That* was about being too competitive. It's the I've-got-to-win attitude like Michael's that sours a sport."

"Michael doesn't have a bad attitude," Lee Anne said. "And he's right. Riders in Germany *don't* have to scrounge for everything."

Lee Anne stood and faced the others, her cheeks flushed. "Michael's had to work hard to get where he is. He's sacrificed everything. If he doesn't do well at this show, he might lose Curio, too. The stress is really eating at him."

Nancy touched her friend's elbow. "Hey, we understand, Lee Anne."

Tears pricked Lee Anne's eyes. "You can't possibly understand. You have no idea how hard it's been for him. I'm sorry. I've got to go find Michael. I'll see you back at the motel room." Picking up her purse, she hurried out of the restaurant.

Bess stood up. "Lee Anne!" she called.

"Let her go," Nancy said. "She and Michael may need some time together."

"We can get a cab," Ned said. "I, for one, would like to stay and enjoy a juicy steak."

Gunter raised his soda glass. "I second the motion. Bess?"

With a sigh, she sat down and clinked glasses

with him. "A toast to a pleasant evening. I think we'll have one now that Michael's gone. He really is a downer."

Nancy had to agree. Still, Michael obviously *was* under a lot of pressure. Though, Nancy wondered, what had Lee Anne meant when she'd said Michael might lose Curio? Did it mean he was so eager to win that he'd be desperate enough to injure or steal a competitor's horse?

"Nan?" Ned's voice broke into her thoughts. "What are you going to order?"

Nancy smiled. "How about the answers to my questions?"

"I know it's a cliché," Nancy said to Ned as they stepped into the motel lobby. "But that really was the perfect ending to a great evening."

The dinner had been delicious. Since Gunter had to be up early to prepare for his ride, he and Bess had taken a cab from the restaurant. Ned and Nancy had chosen to take a leisurely walk back to the motel. It had given them time to catch up on how Ned's college classes were coming along this semester. Nancy filled Ned in on the news from River Heights.

"The dinner was great," Ned said, "except for Michael's outburst, of course."

"Yes. But that didn't seem to ruin anyone's appetite." Nancy yawned. "Well, it's almost eleven, and I'm bushed."

"Me, too. Chasing bad guys is hard work."
After saying good night, Ned and Nancy headed
for their rooms. Nancy unlocked the door to her
room, opened it, and peeked in. The light between the still-made beds was on. The sound of
running water came from the bathroom. She shut
the door, slipped off her shoes, and fell backward
on one of the beds, exhausted.

Bess came out of the bathroom, dressed in
pajamas, her face washed. "You made it." She
plunked down next to Nancy. "I thought maybe
you'd fallen in a ditch."

"No. It was a beautiful night to walk. Also, it
was nice to be with Ned and talk about friends
and school—anything but horses."

Nancy laughed. "Did you and Gunter have a
good time? He seems really nice, and his stories
about life in Germany were interesting."

"We had a great time—after Michael and Lee
Anne left."

Propping herself up on her elbows, Nancy
glanced at the other bed. "Lee Anne's not
back?"

"No. And there was no message."

"I hope she's okay." Nancy felt a pang of
anxiety.

Bess wrinkled her nose. "Maybe Michael
bored her to death."

"Don't say that." Jumping off the bed, Nancy
picked up her purse.

"Where are you going?" Bess asked.

"*We* are going back to the showgrounds, so get dressed."

"Why?" Bess picked up a pair of jeans she'd draped over the bed.

"To look for Lee Anne. If Michael is the thief who attempted to steal the horse, or if he's involved in any way, Lee Anne could be in trouble."

Ten minutes later Nancy and Bess were showing their parking passes to the guard at the front gate. Nancy wondered if they'd beefed up security since the attempted theft. Though even if they had, the person who'd tried to take Sweet and Klean probably had a legitimate pass.

Nancy parked in front of Barn C. There were no other cars in the lot outside. The door at the end of the barn was open, and the aisle was dark.

"Are you sure we should go in?" Bess asked.

"It does look deserted," Nancy replied. She opened the car door and stepped out. "Still, I'd sleep a lot better if I knew where Lee Anne was."

Bess jumped out to join her. "Me, too."

The barn was illuminated by dim ceiling lights. Slowly Nancy walked down the aisle, glancing into each stall. The horses were quietly munching hay or sleeping in the straw.

"Let's check to see if Gilly's awake," Nancy whispered. "She may know where Lee Anne is."

Nancy went over to the stall Gilly slept in. The

cot was neatly made up as if no one had been in it yet.

"She's not here," Nancy said.

"Neither is Aristocrat." Bess was peering into his stall. "Maybe she's out walking him or something."

"At this hour?" Nancy hurried over and peered into the horse's stall. The door was open, the stall empty.

"What are you guys doing here?" a voice asked.

Startled, Nancy jumped a foot, and Bess squeaked. Gilly was striding down the aisle.

"Looking for Lee Anne," Nancy replied. She gestured to the empty stall. "Where's Aristocrat?"

Gilly's eyes widened in alarm. "What do you mean? I just checked on him," she said as she rushed over. When she saw the empty stall, she clasped a hand over her mouth, stifling a cry. "He's gone. Someone must have taken him!"

# 7

## A Secret

Nancy put a hand on Gilly's arm. "Don't panic. Maybe Klaus moved Aristocrat."

Quickly Nancy, Gilly, and Bess raced up and down the aisle, checking every stall. There was no sign of the stallion.

"This is terrible," Gilly moaned. "Klaus will kill me. I left for just a second to get a soda, but some of my friends were hanging around at the little coffee shop that's open all night, and we started talking and . . ." Her voice trailed off, and she hung her head.

"How long were you gone?" Nancy asked.

"No longer than twenty, maybe twenty-five minutes." Gilly wrung her hands. "I've got to call Klaus."

Bess patted her shoulder. "Maybe there's a simple explanation," she said in a reassuring voice, but the look she gave Nancy was full of concern.

"In the meantime we'll alert Security," Nancy told her. "There's a guard checking the cars coming in and out of the grounds. Maybe he saw someone enter the barn."

"Maybe," Gilly repeated, but she didn't sound convinced. When she left to call Klaus Schaudt from the barn's pay phone, Nancy and Bess headed for the booth at the gate. The security guard paged Texel at home, then called for two guards to report to the barn.

While they waited for the chief of security to show up, Nancy and Bess told the guard at the gate, Fred Dunlevy, about the missing horse. "Did anyone leave with a horse in the last half hour?" Nancy asked him.

Fred shook his head. "No trailers or vans went by here. So the horse must be on the grounds somewhere. We'll find him."

"Gilly will be glad to hear that," Bess said.

Five minutes later Texel roared into the show-grounds, gravel flying from beneath his truck tires. "Get in," he growled, swinging open the passenger door.

Without a word, Bess and Nancy scrambled inside. Texel wasn't wearing his cowboy hat, and his thinning hair stuck up as if he'd just gotten out of bed.

"You girls better not have dragged me from a sound sleep in air-conditioned comfort for nothin'." He cast a disgruntled look at them. "I mean, this isn't part two of your Halloween prank, is it?"

"No," Nancy said. "Klaus Schaudt's stallion, Aristocrat, is missing. We checked every stall in Barn C. His groom says she was away from him for only about twenty minutes."

Texel grunted, then took a mug from a cup holder on the dashboard. "Schaudt's stallion, huh?" he repeated after taking a sip. "Well, we'd better find him, or I'll never hear the end of it."

The barn was ablaze with light. When the three went inside, Gilly and two guards were checking all the stalls.

Texel was about to say something when a loud voice barked, "Have you found him? Have you found my horse?"

Nancy turned to see Schaudt stride down the aisle toward them. He was elegantly dressed in a navy blazer over a white shirt and a canary yellow vest.

"Mr. Schaudt," Texel said in his own booming voice. "We have not found your horse yet, but I have alerted my entire security crew. We will have an answer for you as soon as possible."

Schaudt didn't break stride. Scowling, he marched up to Gilly, who seemed to shrink into the concrete.

"Miss Phillips has some explaining to do," Schaudt said, his steely gaze riveted on her. "Like why she was gone long enough for this to happen."

"I just went to get a soda," Gilly said, her voice a whisper.

Schaudt's gaze didn't waver. "Then you should have had someone cover for you I warned you not to leave Aristocrat. There have been too many unexplained incidents." His eyes swung to Texel.

Nancy exhaled. She hadn't realized how tense she had become, even though Schaudt hadn't been reprimanding her.

"We're working on those incidents," Texel said. "We've had a guard at the front gate all evening. He reports that no horses were transported from the showgrounds. That means your stallion's here somewhere."

Schaudt took a step toward Texel, his back ramrod-straight. "Then why aren't you looking for my horse?" he asked, his tone accusing.

Without a word, Texel met the other man's gaze. "We are," he finally drawled. "If you have a photo of the horse, it would help greatly."

"I brought one just for that purpose." Schaudt plucked one from his jacket pocket, handed it to

Texel, then scowled at Gilly. "I'm not through with you yet, Miss Phillips. But right now I need to look for my horse."

Whipping around, he marched out of the barn.

Gilly burst into tears. Covering her eyes, she raced in the opposite direction.

For a second no one said a word. Then Texel waved the photo at the two guards. "Look at this; then check *every* stall in *every* barn. I'm going to call the county and state police. If we don't find Aristocrat, I'll fax them a copy of this photo so they can keep their eyes peeled for any vans on the highway this late at night."

As Texel and the guards were leaving, Lee Anne and Michael came into the barn from the parking lot.

"What's going on?" Michael asked. "Klaus called me and told me to come over here. He said there was a problem."

Michael and Lee Anne were still dressed in the clothes they'd worn to dinner. Since it was almost midnight, Nancy wondered where they'd been since they left the restaurant.

"Aristocrat's gone," Nancy explained.

Lee Anne blinked. "Gone?"

"What do you mean he's gone?" Rushing over to the stallion's stall, Michael looked inside, then turned to Nancy. "Where's Gilly? What's being done to find the horse?"

"Klaus bawled Gilly out, and she ran off,"

Nancy explained. "Klaus and the guards are checking all the barns. Texel went to call the state and local police."

"Poor Gilly." Lee Anne bit her lip.

"Poor Gilly—nothing," Michael snapped. "Klaus *should* have chewed her out. It's her job to watch Aristocrat."

While he talked, he walked up and down the aisle, peering into the other stalls. "At least the other horses are okay." He ran his fingers through his thick hair in a gesture of frustration. "Man, I don't need this. I've got to be ready for my dressage test in the morning."

"You go and get some sleep," Lee Anne told him. "I'll stay here."

"Are you sure?" Michael glanced down the aisle, his expression anxious. Nancy couldn't tell if he felt guilty or just worried because the stallion was gone.

"Yes," Lee Anne reassured him. "Klaus will understand."

Michael snorted. "True. One thing Klaus does understand is winning. Well, I'm out of here." His gaze flicked to Nancy before he hurried away.

Nancy faced Lee Anne. "Bess and I were worried when you didn't come back to the room. Where did you and Michael go?"

Lee Anne seemed to grow tense. "We just went somewhere to talk. Why?"

65

"Hey, don't get so uptight," Bess said. "It was late, and we didn't know where you were. We came to the barn to look for you."

"Oh." Lee Anne's shoulders relaxed. "Sorry. Today's just been so crazy. I mean, when I invited you two to come to the show, I never dreamed all this would happen. Then on top of it, Michael's been so upset. I've never seen him like this." When she looked at Nancy, tears glistened in her eyes.

"Do you think something's bothering him other than the usual show pressures?" Nancy probed.

"If it is, he's not telling me." Lee Anne sniffled. "And now this . . ." She waved to Aristocrat's empty stall. "What a nightmare."

Putting one arm around Lee Anne's shoulders, Bess gave her friend a hug. "Cheer up. Fortunately, you invited a great detective and her best friend to the show. We'll help find Aristocrat."

"Thanks." Lee Anne wiped her eyes with her fingers.

"Which means we'd better do something." Nancy thought for a minute. The guards were searching the other barns, so that was covered. She thought about the missing gray trailer. "I think we should check the parking lot. Someone could have loaded Aristocrat into a van or a trailer, just waiting for a chance to drive out."

Bess nodded. "That makes sense."

66

"Gilly keeps one of those big flashlights by her cot," Lee Anne said. "Poor Gilly," she said as she went to retrieve it. "Klaus is one of the greatest riders and trainers, but he treats his horses a lot better than he treats his human help."

Flicking on the flashlight, Lee Anne led the way from the barn to the parking lot. As the trio went from trailer to trailer, Bess huddled close to Nancy. "I don't want some man in one of those masks to jump out at me," she confessed.

A half hour later they'd worked their way to the chain-link fence that circled the outer perimeter of the lot. Nancy frowned in frustration. "I think we looked in every vehicle here. No sign of Aristocrat."

"No *sound* of him either," Lee Anne added. "Most horses alone in a trailer are going to stomp or whinny. This place is so silent it's creepy."

Taking the flashlight, Nancy aimed it around the lot just to make sure they hadn't missed anything. When she ran the beam along the fence, her heartbeat quickened. "Look!"

She pointed the light at one section of fence. The metal links had been cut and the fence peeled back.

Lee Anne gasped. "Someone cut a big hole in the chain links!"

Nancy moved closer to inspect it. "Big enough to lead a horse through." Eyes on the ground, Nancy made her way through the hole. The beam picked up two hoofprints in the mud. On the other side of the fence Nancy could see a field. When she swung the light around, she noticed flattened grass in two parallel lines where a vehicle had been driven.

She glanced over her shoulder at Bess and Lee Anne. "Looks as if someone led a horse through here, which means trouble. If it was Aristocrat, it means the stallion's not on the grounds anymore."

"Do you think he was stolen?" Lee Anne gasped.

"That's what it looks like. We'd better alert Security."

With Nancy leading the way, the three girls hurried back to the barn. Texel and Klaus were standing in the middle of the aisle. Klaus was scowling and waving an arm in the air. Nancy gulped. He wasn't going to like the latest news.

Quickly she told them what she and her friends had found.

Klaus's eyes narrowed. "So you were wrong about my horse being on the grounds," he said to Texel. "It sounds to me as if he's been stolen!"

Texel rubbed his forehead. Pulling out his walkie-talkie, he relayed the information to his men and told them to alert the state and county police. "Now show us this break in the fence," he said to Nancy.

"Lee Anne and Bess will take you there. I'm

going to find Gilly." Nancy looked sideways at Klaus.

The trainer shook his head and made a noise of disgust. Then he headed down the aisle after Texel. "No more delays. Let's find my horse," he barked.

When they had left, Nancy thought about where Gilly might have gone. She remembered the groom saying she'd met with some friends at the coffee shop. Nancy was about to leave the barn, when she heard a soft sniffing coming from one of the stalls.

She held her breath and listened. Someone was crying. Moving quietly, she made her way toward the sound, which was coming from the tack stall.

She peered inside. Gilly was slumped on a tack trunk, head in her hands.

Nancy knew she must have heard everything they'd said. "Hey, Gilly." Nancy sat beside her on the trunk. "It's not all bad news. Whoever took Aristocrat couldn't have gotten much of a head start, and Texel has alerted the county and state police, so they can be on the lookout."

Tears glistening in her eyes, Gilly looked up at her. "It's not just that," she whispered hoarsely. Grabbing Nancy's wrist, she squeezed tightly, her eyes wide. "You've got to help me, Nancy. I don't know who else to trust. I know something about Aristocrat's disappearance!"

# 8

## A Risky Meeting

"Do you know who stole Aristocrat?" Nancy asked Gilly.

"No, but this morning, when I gave Aristocrat a bath, I couldn't find his scar," Gilly said.

Nancy frowned, puzzled. Then the thud of rubber soles on the concrete aisle made her look up.

Gilly inhaled sharply. "Someone's coming." Bending closer to Nancy, she whispered hurriedly, "Meet me here at five-thirty. I've got to feed early, then braid Curio."

The footsteps moved closer. Gilly grew rigid. "If something happens to me, look for the scar on Aristocrat's hock."

"There you are." Klaus stepped into the doorway, blocking the dim light. Hands on his hips, he eyed Nancy, then Gilly. The groom jumped to her feet.

"Don't look so worried," Klaus stated. "I came to apologize for blaming you for Aristocrat's disappearance." He spoke slowly, as if the words were hard to say. "I was distraught. I know you love Aristocrat as much as I do."

"I do," Gilly said, her voice wavering. She glanced at Nancy. "I need to find out what Security's doing. I'll see you later." Excusing herself, she went around Klaus.

Nancy stood up. "I'd better help, too."

Klaus extended a hand to stop her from leaving. "Miss Drew, if I may speak with you for a minute. Mr. Texel told me you are a detective. I am in need of help. I do not trust Security to find my horse. Perhaps you could be of assistance?"

Nancy hesitated. She'd witnessed how overbearing Klaus Schaudt could be. But he *had* apologized to Gilly, something that must have been difficult for him.

"I am very worried about my horse," he continued. "Not only is Aristocrat valuable, but I raised him from a foal. He is family."

"I understand," Nancy said. Maybe there was a soft side to the trainer after all. "And I'll do whatever I can, though I think Mr. Texel knows his business."

"Humph." Klaus threw back his shoulders.

"My belief is that the security crew is behind the theft."

Nancy's eyebrows shot up. "What makes you say that?" she asked, startled by his statement.

"Because the theft was obviously an inside job. The thief must know the showgrounds, as well as the guards' schedules. Otherwise the person would not have been able to steal such a large animal without someone seeing him."

Nancy nodded. Klaus's observation about the thief being someone on the inside was similar to her own hunch, but she'd been so intent on Michael as a suspect that she'd never thought about the guards.

"In fact," Klaus said, lowering his voice, "it is my belief that they are operating a theft ring. There are several horses here as valuable as Aristocrat. He was just the unlucky target."

"It would be interesting to find out if there have been other thefts at past shows," Nancy said.

Klaus dismissed her suggestion with a wave of his hand. "That wouldn't prove anything. Many of the shows here are smaller, attracting only local horses that wouldn't be worth stealing." He straightened. "So. We will work together. Now I need to find out what Mr. Texel has discovered. Good evening."

As she watched Klaus leave, Nancy thought about his theory. It made sense. Still, she wasn't going to drop Michael as a possible suspect. As soon as she saw Lee Anne, she would ask her if the two had been together all evening.

Then there was Gilly's cryptic message about Aristocrat's scar. Whatever Gilly knew, she obviously hadn't wanted to share the information with Klaus.

Nancy checked her watch. It was one o'clock in the morning. In four and a half hours she had to meet Gilly. Then maybe she'd find out what the groom knew about the theft of Aristocrat.

"I'm going to sleep until noon," Bess said, flopping down on the bed. She was back in her pajamas. "So don't anybody dare wake me up."

Lee Anne plopped down on her bed and began to take off her shoes. "I wish I could sleep that late. But I've got to meet Michael at the barn at seven-thirty. He's got a nine o'clock test."

Good, Nancy thought as she headed into the bathroom to brush her teeth. She hoped no one else would be at the barn when she met Gilly. She could set the alarm for five and sneak out of the room. Lee Anne and Bess were so tired they wouldn't hear her.

"So did you and Michael get to talk tonight?" Nancy asked Lee Anne when she came out of the bathroom.

"Yeah. He was pretty upset when he left the restaurant."

"Where did you go?" Bess mumbled, her cheek pressed into the pillow.

Lee Anne stopped in the middle of pulling her nightgown on. "Why are you so interested in what Michael and I did?" she asked, her eyes shifting from Bess to Nancy.

"We just hoped you two had a good time," Nancy said quickly. She didn't want Lee Anne to know about her suspicion that Michael might have something to do with the theft.

Lee Anne yanked the nightgown over her head. "Well, we just drove around and talked," she said. "And I was with him all evening." Grabbing her brush off the dresser, she stomped into the bathroom, shutting the door behind her.

"Well, that settles that." Bess yawned and snuggled under the covers. "Michael can't be our thief. See you around lunchtime," she mumbled and promptly fell asleep.

Nancy took off her skirt and top. Before crawling in beside Bess, she put on a clean T-shirt and laid her jeans at the foot of the bed. When the alarm went off, it would still be dark and she'd be groggy from lack of sleep. She wasn't giving herself much time to get to the barn, so she needed to hit the ground running.

*Brrring.* The persistent sound woke Nancy from a deep sleep. Beside her, Bess mumbled something about Gunter. Reaching up, Nancy hit the alarm's Off button.

She groaned softly. Four hours of sleep was not enough.

She slipped out of bed and tiptoed to the bathroom, grabbing her jeans on the way. After splashing cold water on her face and brushing her teeth, she felt a little more awake.

Ten minutes later she shut the door quietly behind her. She was tempted to go to Ned's room and wake him up. Going to the barn alone after all that had happened wasn't the smartest idea she'd ever had.

She knew she had to see Gilly alone, though. The girl had clearly stated that Nancy was the only person she trusted. If she brought Ned along, the groom might be reluctant to confide in her.

The lobby was well lighted. The clerk said good morning and pointed out a tray of pastries and a pitcher of orange juice. Nancy grabbed a blueberry muffin and a glass of juice, then headed for her Mustang.

The sky was gray, the air cool. While Nancy drove to the showgrounds, she munched on the muffin and sorted through everything that had happened since they'd arrived. If Lee Anne was telling the truth, then Michael hadn't stolen Aristocrat last night. Still, that didn't mean he wasn't working with an accomplice.

Nancy rolled her eyes, suddenly realizing how dead set she was on making Michael the bad guy. Maybe she wanted to find him guilty because she didn't like his arrogance.

A sleepy-eyed guard halted her at the front gate of the showgrounds. He was the same man she and Bess had talked to the night before.

"Good morning, Fred," Nancy said. "Any more news?"

He shook his head. "The only good news is I'm out of here in an hour. Texel wants us all to work double shifts, but I need some shut-eye."

He checked her pass, then asked, "What brings you here so early on a Saturday morning? The sun's not even up."

"I have to help feed the horses. One of the riders has an early test." A thought suddenly crossed Nancy's mind. "You didn't see a dented old station wagon come in here last night, did you?"

"Nope. Can't say I did. Though another guard, Andy Brackett, relieved me so I could get some coffee. I'll ask him."

"Thanks," Nancy said, and drove in. No other cars were parked in front of Barn C. When Nancy glanced to her right, she saw a few solitary people moving around the showgrounds.

After locking the Mustang, Nancy went into the barn. The aisle was empty, the barn quiet. Nancy walked past several stalls. The horses' heads were down, and they were munching hay, so Nancy knew Gilly had fed them already. She peeked into the stall next to Aristocrat's. The cot was neatly made. Since Gilly had said something about braiding Curio, Nancy headed for his stall.

When she reached Curio's stall, the handsome bay started at the sight of her. Head high, he snorted loudly. A lead line dangled from his halter, and when he swung his head, Nancy saw a needle and thread hanging from a half-finished braid in his mane.

She pushed open the door, which wasn't latched. "Gilly?" she called. She couldn't believe the groom would have left without securing the door.

Curio pawed at the straw. Hand outstretched, Nancy went up to him. "Easy, guy," she crooned. Nancy grasped the lead line. Reaching up, she smoothed his neck, still talking soothingly. With a toss of his head, Curio swung his hindquarters to the right.

Nancy froze. A denim-clad leg, half hidden in the straw, extended into the middle of the stall.

Nancy darted around Curio's head. A girl was crumpled in the straw, her back propped against the wall. Her eyes were closed, and blood trickled down her forehead.

Nancy gasped. It was Gilly!

# 9

## A Bad-Luck Horseshoe

Nancy knew she had to act quickly. She jumped up, startling Curio. The bay nickered nervously, then banged the mesh door with his hoof. Nancy realized she'd better get him out of the stall and away from Gilly.

Speaking in a calm voice, Nancy grabbed the dangling lead line. "Okay, Curio, let's put you in Aristocrat's stall. Then I'll call for help."

She opened the door, and Curio leaped out. "Easy. Easy." Nancy steered him to the empty stall. A scuffling noise behind her made her whirl.

A dark figure darted from a stall and disappeared down the cross aisle. The movement was so sudden that Nancy thought she was seeing things. But Curio was staring, too.

Quickly she put the horse in the stall and latched the door. Then she raced down the aisle. The sound of receding footsteps came from the other side of the barn. Nancy dashed down the cross aisle, but when she got to the other side, no one was there. Then she heard a car engine rev up.

Nancy reached the open barn door just in time to see a car speed past the guard's booth and disappear from the showgrounds, dust and gravel pluming out from the back tires. The morning light was so dim she couldn't see the license plate. Still, Nancy thought she recognized the vehicle as the old station wagon Michael had driven the night before.

There was no time to think about what she'd seen. She had to get help for Gilly.

Nancy raced to the guard's booth. Fred Dunlevy stepped outside to meet her. "What's going on?"

"Call an ambulance," she puffed. "There's been an accident. One of the grooms is hurt!"

Fred hustled over to the phone while Nancy told him what she'd discovered. After he'd finished calling, she asked him about the car that had left.

"It roared by so fast that I couldn't identify it,"

Fred said apologetically. "I'd stepped out of the booth on the other side to check the pass of a van coming in."

Nancy considered what Fred had said. She would be the only witness, and she wasn't at all sure about what she had seen.

Ten minutes later Texel arrived, followed by the ambulance crew.

"She's been hit on the head," Texel told Nancy as he left the stall to make room for the three emergency medical technicians, who bustled in with trauma kits.

Nancy was leaning against the doorjamb. She was exhausted from lack of sleep and from worrying about Gilly.

"Now show me the horse that was with her when you found her."

"Over here." Nancy led Texel to Aristocrat's stall. Curio stared at them, stalks of hay sticking out of his mouth. "Gilly was braiding him for the show. See?" Nancy pointed to the needle and thread still dangling from his mane.

Texel rubbed his chin. Shadows ringed his eyes, and Nancy figured he hadn't gotten much sleep, either. "Can you hold the horse for me? I want to check his hooves," he asked her.

"What for?"

Texel swung around to look at her. "Now, Miss Drew, haven't you figured out what happened yet? This here horse must have kicked that girl.

Not much of a contest when it's a thousand pounds of critter versus a hundred pounds of human."

Nancy's jaw dropped. "Curio? He wouldn't hurt a flea."

"I've squashed plenty of fleas myself, and I'm a pretty nice guy." Texel flipped open the latch. "Get a rope. I want to have something to report to the police when they come."

Speaking softly, Nancy went into the stall. Curio nuzzled her palm, looking for a treat. She knew there was no way the horse would have purposely kicked Gilly.

"I'll pick up the hoof for you," Nancy said after attaching the lead. "It will prove that Curio's a lamb. He would never have kicked Gilly."

"Maybe not on purpose."

Standing next to Curio's right flank, Nancy ran her hand down his hind leg. Curio immediately picked it up. She cradled his hoof in her left palm. Bending, Texel inspected the horseshoe.

"There's our proof." He pointed to a crusted brown spot. "Looks like blood to me. A steel shoe combined with a powerful kick to the head would knock anyone out. I'm surprised it didn't kill her."

Slowly Nancy set down Curio's hoof. "Something must have scared him, or else it was just a freak accident," she protested.

"Maybe. We'll let the police decide," Texel said as he left the stall. From outside the barn Nancy could hear the shrill whine of sirens. She gave Curio one last pat, then unhooked the lead. As she latched the door, Texel said, "Now, is there anything you want to tell me before the cops get here and start stomping around?" He studied her face. "Like what you were doing here at five-thirty in the morning after being up almost all night chasing horse thieves?"

Nancy hesitated. She wasn't ready to tell him that Gilly had wanted to confide something about the theft of Aristocrat. If Curio had accidentally kicked Gilly, that information wouldn't matter. But she did think it was important to tell him about the person who had fled from the barn. He or she could be a witness—or maybe could have provoked the horse into kicking the groom.

"I came to help Gilly get the horses ready. When I realized she was hurt, I knew I'd better move Curio," Nancy explained. "I was leading him down the aisle when I saw someone dart out of a stall and run around the corner to the other side of the barn. It all happened so fast that I couldn't see who it was. The person got away in a car that I sort of recognized."

Texel raised one eyebrow, but when someone came into the barn and hollered, "Texel, what's going on around this place?" he put a finger to his lips and said, "Finish telling me later."

Turning, he faced two uniformed police officers striding down the aisle. One was a woman with a badge over her pocket. The other was an older man who had hailed Texel.

"Just drumming up a little business for you, Yates," Texel greeted the older officer. "Only I think this was an accident."

"Yeah?" Yates shook hands with Texel, then slapped him on the back. "So you wrapped up the case for us, huh?"

Texel gestured to the stall. "The girl's in there. The EMTs are getting ready to transport her to the hospital. She got a nasty blow on the head. Looks like a horse kicked her."

"Any witnesses?" the other officer asked, pulling a pad from her shirt pocket.

"Not yet. Miss Drew here found her."

"Did someone call Klaus Schaudt?" Nancy asked Texel.

He shook his head. "I'll leave that up to the police. I don't need that man breathing down my neck just yet."

"Hey, let us in!" Nancy heard an irate voice boom down the aisle. Michael and Lee Anne stood in the doorway of the barn, where they'd been stopped by a police officer.

"That's Michael Raines," Nancy told Texel. "He's Curio's rider. The girl is Lee Anne Suna. I think you met them last night when Aristocrat was stolen. They both work for Klaus."

"Right." Texel stuck a toothpick in his mouth and began to chew on it. Nancy wondered if he was pondering the same thing she was—was there a connection between last night's theft and this morning's incident?

Just then one of the EMTs came out of the stall. "We're ready to transport her, but first I need to find out a few things about the patient."

"Lee Anne and Michael would be the ones to ask." Nancy pointed to the pair, who were talking to the police officer at the door. The EMT headed toward them at a brisk pace.

Five minutes later the other two EMTs brought Gilly out. She was strapped to a stretcher, her face as white as the bulky bandage wrapped around her forehead.

Nancy bit her lip, holding back a sob. Would Gilly be okay?

Turning, she followed them down the aisle. She wanted to tell Lee Anne and Michael what had happened, but the EMT was still talking to them. As Nancy approached, the EMT put away his sheet and left with the others. When the ambulance roared off, Lee Anne turned to Nancy.

"Gilly's really hurt!" she exclaimed, the blood rushing from her face. "But what . . . how?"

Michael glowered at the officer. "What do you mean we can't go in the barn right now? What authority do the police have to keep me from my horses? I've got to compete this morning."

"Texel thinks Curio might have accidentally kicked Gilly," Nancy explained. "There was blood on his horseshoe."

For a second Michael stood speechless. Then he snorted. "That's crazy. I'm going to find Klaus. He'll straighten this out." Turning, he stomped off.

Nancy watched him go. He'd never once mentioned Gilly, she realized.

"I can't believe it," Lee Anne said. "First Aristocrat, now Gilly." She raised her eyes to Nancy. "Do you think she'll be okay?"

"I wish I knew." Nancy stepped outside the barn and walked away from the doorway, then motioned for Lee Anne to come closer. "I have to tell you that I think I saw Michael's station wagon roar out of here right after I found Gilly."

Lee Anne stared at Nancy in disbelief. "So what if it did? What's that got to do with Curio kicking Gilly?"

"Do you really think Curio kicked her?" Nancy asked.

Lee Anne shook her head, but then her eyes narrowed. "Wait a minute. You don't think Michael had anything to do with Gilly's accident, do you? That's even crazier than accusing Curio!"

"Nancy." Texel came striding out of the barn. Lee Anne glanced from Nancy to Texel. Without another word, she left in a huff.

Nancy just stared as Lee Anne stomped away. If she said anything to Texel about Michael, Lee Anne would never forgive her.

Taking Nancy's elbow, Texel steered her farther from the barn. "What else were you going to tell me?" He kept his voice low.

Nancy took a deep breath. No matter what Lee Anne's reaction was, Nancy had to inform Texel about the station wagon.

"The car I saw zooming out of the parking lot was an old station wagon. It looked like the one Michael Raines was driving when we all went out to dinner last night."

"Did you see it when you first drove in?" Texel asked.

"No. But it was pretty dark, and the wagon could have been parked in the lot with all the trailers and vans."

"Good." Texel dipped his head.

He was about to go, but Nancy stopped him with a hand on his arm. "Now you have to tell me what's going on," she said.

"That's fair. I told the officers you'd seen someone run from the barn, so just in case the horse didn't kick the girl, we're checking around." Texel eyed her. "Do you have any idea why someone might want to hurt Gilly?"

Nancy nodded. It was too late to keep Gilly's secret. "Last night Gilly begged me to meet her this morning. She said she knew something about the theft of Aristocrat."

Texel jerked his head up in surprise. "The theft?"

"Yes. Only when I got here it was too late to find out what she meant."

"That complicates things." Texel rubbed his hand over his chin, scraping against his rough whiskers. "So you think there's a connection?"

"I wish I knew," Nancy said, suddenly gloomy. A horse had been stolen and a girl knocked unconscious, and she had no idea who was responsible.

"Hey, Texel!" Yates hollered.

Nancy and Texel swung around to see what was going on. Yates was standing in the doorway of the stall that High Hills used as a tack room. "I think I've got something."

Nancy and Texel hurried to the stall. Yates stood in front of a tack trunk. Printed on the side of the trunk was a name: Michael Raines, High Hills Farm. With gloved fingers, Yates reached behind the tack box and pulled out a rasp—a long metal bar with a rough surface. When he held it up, Nancy gasped.

The edge of the rasp was covered with blood.

# 10

## *Caught*

"We should be able to match the blood on this rasp with that of the victim," Yates explained. "Maybe we'll even be lucky and lift some finger-prints."

Texel looked at Nancy. "And the tack box belongs to Michael Raines? Interesting. Nancy, tell Sergeant Yates what you saw this morning."

"So the person might have run from this stall?" Yates asked after Nancy repeated her story.

Nancy nodded.

"I think we'd better find Raines," Yates told Texel. The police officer was carefully putting the rasp into an evidence bag.

"Let me in!" an insistent voice resounded along the aisle. Nancy recognized Klaus Schaudt's voice. "Texel! Tell this officer I demand to be let into my barn."

Texel jerked his head toward the bellowing. "That's Klaus Schaudt. You'd better tell your officer to let him pass," he told Yates.

A minute later Klaus strode down the aisle, Michael and Lee Anne behind him. "What is the meaning of this?" he demanded.

"Mr. Raines," Texel said, ignoring Klaus. "This is Sergeant Yates from the county police department. He needs to ask you a few questions."

Yates pointed into the stall. "Is this your trunk?"

"Yes," Michael said without even looking into the stall.

"Do you keep a metal rasp in your tack box?"

Michael's expression grew wary. "Yes. Sometimes I need to file a hoof or reset a shoe if a farrier isn't available."

"What are you getting at?" Klaus insisted.

Yates ignored Klaus. "Mr. Raines, where were you between four and five-thirty this morning?"

Michael's wariness changed to annoyance. "In my room. Asleep."

"Alone?"

Michael set his mouth in a firm line. "I don't think I need to answer any more questions."

Just then the female officer came jogging into the barn and motioned Yates over. Nancy watched as they had a whispered conversation before Yates turned back to Michael.

"Mr. Raines, we'd like you to come down to the police station to answer some questions."

Klaus threw his shoulders back. "Not until you tell us what's going on."

"It seems we have a contradiction here," Yates said. "Mr. Raines claims he was in his motel early this morning. However, a temporary guard at the booth, Andy Brackett, reports checking his pass at exactly five this morning as Michael drove in."

All the blood drained from Michael's face. "That can't be," he replied.

"No!" Lee Anne clapped a hand over her mouth, stifling a cry. Nancy looked away, unable to face Lee Anne. Michael was rude and overly competitive, but would he go after Gilly?

As the two officers led Michael away, Lee Anne gave Nancy an anguished look. Then she ran after Klaus, who was right behind the officers, declaring, "This is absurd! We'll have you back in time for your first test, Michael."

When they left, Texel muttered, "What a nightmare."

Nancy agreed as a sudden wave of sadness and exhaustion hit her. Just then she saw Ned silhouetted in the barn doorway. Quickly she ran to greet him. She had never been so happy to see anyone in her life.

\* \* \*

"Lee Anne wants us to pick her up at the police station," Bess said at breakfast.

After leaving the barn with Ned, Nancy had headed back to the motel for a shower. When Bess woke up, Nancy had explained everything to her. Bess had immediately called the police station and asked for Lee Anne, who was waiting there for news about Michael.

Now it was ten o'clock, and Nancy, Ned, and Bess were waiting to be served pancakes in the motel coffee shop.

"I didn't think Lee Anne would want to see me again," Nancy replied.

"It wasn't your fault you saw the station wagon leaving," Ned pointed out. "And you didn't find the rasp behind the tack trunk."

Nancy sighed. "I know."

"Lee Anne says the police are trying to connect Michael to the horse theft," Bess said.

Nancy nodded. "Texel said he was going to toss that theory out to Yates. After all, if Michael did attack Gilly, the police need to figure out why."

"If he was involved in Aristocrat's theft and Gilly found out, she could have ruined his riding career forever." Ned sipped his orange juice.

"That certainly would give him a motive to assault Gilly," Bess agreed glumly. "I'm just glad she's okay."

An hour earlier they'd called the hospital. Gilly was still unconscious, but there was no internal damage and she was expected to recover soon.

"Let's hope Lee Anne will tell us where she and Michael were last night," Nancy said. "If he has an alibi for the time of the theft, he could be cleared."

Just then the pancakes were served. They smelled heavenly.

Half an hour later they reached the police station. Lee Anne met them at the front door. Her eyes were red from crying.

"The police haven't charged Michael with any crime," she explained. "But Klaus says they will. He's already called a lawyer."

"I'm so sorry." Bess handed her a tissue.

Lee Anne blew her nose. "They matched the blood on the rasp with Gilly's. They also found Michael's prints on the rasp handle"—she raised bloodshot eyes to Nancy—"but Michael says he was in his room asleep."

"If he was alone, there's no one to back up his alibi," Ned said.

"But why would he go after Gilly?" Lee Anne countered. "That doesn't make sense."

Putting an arm around Lee Anne's shoulder, Bess led her toward Nancy's Mustang. "Come on. You need something to eat and then a nap. None of us got much sleep last night."

Ned grinned sheepishly. "I did. I slept through everything."

Nancy yawned. "Good. You can drive *and* think. My brain's numb."

"Don't say that, Nancy." Lee Anne stopped and faced her. "I need you to help prove that Michael's innocent."

"Oh, Lee Anne." Nancy didn't know what to say. The evidence was pretty damaging.

"Nancy?" Bess looked pleadingly at her.

"All right. I'll keep poking around. But if all my snooping only proves that Michael is guilty, I won't lie to the police."

"I don't expect you to," Lee Anne said, some of her old fire returning.

Nancy touched her on the shoulder. "Good, but you have to tell me the truth."

Lee Anne lowered her gaze. "All right."

"I need to know how long you were with Michael last night. And where you went."

Lee Anne's shoulders slumped. "I wasn't with Michael last night," she finally admitted. "When he left the restaurant, he drove off without me. I was too embarrassed to face you guys, so I walked back to the motel."

"But you came into the barn with him after Aristocrat was stolen," Bess pointed out.

"When I got back to the motel, I went to our room and called him, but he didn't answer. When it got late, I grew worried and went to his room to wait. At about twelve-thirty, he came down the hall. I told him we needed to talk. He agreed. But when we got inside his room, the phone rang. It was Klaus, telling us that Aristocrat had been stolen."

"You have no idea where he'd been all that time?" Ned asked.

"He said he'd been doing some thinking about his riding career. That's all."

"Thanks for telling the truth," Nancy said.

"I'm sorry I lied, but I was trying to protect Michael," Lee Anne said. "You kept asking me questions, as if you thought he was involved in the theft. But lying won't help him now."

Nancy was afraid Lee Anne was right.

When they arrived at the motel, Bess got out of the Mustang with her friend. "I'm going to stay here with Lee Anne," she told Nancy and Ned.

"Good idea. We'll head over to the showgrounds to see if Texel found out anything more," Nancy said. "Then I'd like to go see Gilly."

Lee Anne bent down to look in the open car door. "I want to go to the hospital with you, but I've got to be at the barn at four this afternoon to help feed the horses. With Michael and Gilly gone . . ." Her voice faded.

"We'll pick you up about two," Nancy said.

"So you think the key to Gilly's assault is the horse theft?" Ned asked as he drove away.

"It's got to be," Nancy replied. "Gilly wanted to tell me something about the theft. But what could she have known that was so damaging that she was attacked?"

"How about the name of the thief?" Ned guessed.

"That could be it. The problem is, Aristocrat's been gone almost twelve hours. He could be out of the state by now, which means the police may never find him or the thieves. And Texel . . ." Her voice trailed off.

Ned gave her a curious look. "What about Texel?"

She told him Klaus's theory. "What if Klaus is right? What if Texel and his guards are operating a theft ring?"

Ned whistled. "Wow. That would be tough to prove. Do you think Texel could be in on it? He seems as honest as they come."

"I agree," Nancy said. "But right now I'm afraid to trust him. You see, Gilly *did* tell me something."

"What?" Ned braked at a red light.

"She said if anything happened to her, I should check the scar on Aristocrat's hock."

For a second Ned just looked at her. "What do you think she meant?"

"The hock is the joint on the hind leg, I know that much, but what the scar has to do with the theft, I'm not sure." She shook her head. "Unfortunately, I now know what she meant when she said, 'If anything happens to me.'" Nancy shuddered. "That makes me think she knew someone might come after her."

"This is getting dangerous, Nan," Ned said. "I think you need to let the police handle it."

"Not yet. I want to find out something first." Nancy shifted in her car seat to face him. "I have to know if Security is involved."

Ned cocked one eyebrow. "Let me guess," he said in a teasing voice. "That means snooping around their office. Right?"

Nancy grinned. "Yup. We'll do it tonight. If we get caught, we can say we were looking for Texel."

Ned chuckled as he pulled into the showgrounds. "You make it sound so easy."

"Don't worry." Nancy squeezed his fingers. "It'll be a piece of cake."


"I found the guards' schedule," Nancy whispered to Ned. She was rummaging through the top drawer of Texel's desk. Ned was hunting through the file cabinets.

It was after ten o'clock at night. Bess was out with Gunter. Lee Anne had fallen into an exhausted sleep. Earlier, when the four teens visited Gilly, they'd found her unconscious. Still, the doctor remained optimistic.

"When she does regain consciousness," Lee Anne had stated firmly, "she'll clear Michael."

The doctor wasn't sure when Gilly would wake up, however, and Nancy didn't want to wait. If someone else was guilty, she wanted to nab the culprit as soon as possible.

"According to this schedule," Nancy told Ned, "the culprit timed the theft perfectly. He stole Aristocrat at midnight, during the guards' shift change."

"So he must have known their schedule." Ned opened the second file drawer quietly. "Here are the guards' employment records."

"Better check them out." Nancy ran her finger across the schedule, noting who was on guard that night. Quickly she wrote down the names and what times they worked on a small pad.

"Hey. This is interesting," Ned said softly. "One guard, Andy Brackett, used to work for Klaus."

"Really?" Sliding the desk drawer shut, Nancy joined Ned. "How long ago?"

"Just last year."

"Wow." Nancy's mind whirled. "Not only would he know about Aristocrat but he'd know how valuable the horse was."

Flipping open the pad, she glanced at the names of the guards who'd been on duty the night before. When she saw Andy's name, her heart skipped a beat.

"Ned." Nancy held the pad up so Ned could see it in the dim light. "Andy was on duty from midnight until eight o'clock this morning. That means he could have been hanging around right before his shift. No one would have questioned why he was in one of the barns."

"So he could have stolen Aristocrat," Ned said.

Nancy waved the pad excitedly. "It also means one other thing: he was on duty when Gilly was attacked. What if Gilly found out that Andy Brackett had stolen the horse?"

"He would have been able to sneak into the barn and go after her without anyone suspecting," Ned said.

"Right." A gleam came into Nancy's eyes, and she snapped her fingers. "And one more thing— the police officer reported that Andy Brackett was the guard who checked Michael's pass at five o'clock. What if he was lying? What if it wasn't Michael who drove in?"

Ned grinned excitedly. "Then we might be able to prove he's innocent!"

# 11

## A Surprising Twist

"If we can prove Andy Brackett is the culprit, we would clear Michael," Nancy explained. "Now that I think of it, even though Brackett was supposed to be working at midnight, I don't remember seeing him when we searched for Aristocrat." In her excitement, her voice rose.

Ned put a finger to his lips. "Shh. Somebody might hear you."

For a moment they stood and listened for any sounds coming from beyond the closed office door. When Nancy was certain no one had heard her, she whispered, "And maybe Gilly knew one of the guards was the thief. That would explain why she wouldn't confide in Texel."

"But what about Michael's car leaving the barn after Gilly was killed?" Ned asked.

"Maybe Michael was working with Brackett," Nancy said, her spirits sinking. "They may have known each other."

"Or maybe Brackett or someone else used the car to make it look as if Michael was guilty," Ned suggested.

"Good thought." Before tucking the file folder back in the drawer, Nancy wrote down Andy Brackett's address. "We need proof other than Brackett's schedule and the fact that he used to work for Klaus."

"Let's ask Klaus about the guy," Ned said. "Maybe he fired Andy or something. Revenge is a powerful motive."

Nancy closed the drawer. "Klaus will know what kind of a guy Brackett is, too."

For a minute she tried to picture the guard. The man was so unremarkable she barely remembered what he looked like. Short and balding?

When they got back to the motel, Bess was saying good night to Gunter in the lobby. They were laughing together and didn't notice Nancy and Ned until the two came right up to them.

"Oh!" Bess jumped back, blushing. "We didn't see you come in."

"No wonder. You were too busy," Nancy teased. "Did you have fun tonight?"

"A great time." Gunter smiled. "We went

Rollerblading." His expression turned serious. "Though I hear I missed much excitement last night and this morning. I am sorry about your friend Gilly."

"We are, too," Ned said. Bess reluctantly waved goodbye when Gunter headed for his room. "He's so much fun," she said with a sigh.

Ned walked with Nancy and Bess to their room. Bess unlocked the door, then pushed it open and peeked in. "I think Lee Anne is still asleep," she told the others.

"I'll say good night, then," Ned said, yawning. "All that snooping around wore me out, too."

Nancy gave him a quick kiss. "Thanks for your help." When she and Bess went inside, Lee Anne was sitting up in bed. Her hair was tousled, her cheeks pale. Bess had already gone into the bathroom.

"Did you find out anything?" Lee Anne asked.

"Maybe." Nancy sat on the edge of the bed. "But I don't want to get your hopes up, so I'm not going to tell you everything yet. I do need you to answer some questions, though."

Lee Anne nodded sleepily.

"Do you know Andy Brackett?"

She knit her brow. "The name sounds familiar."

"He's one of the security guards. He worked for Klaus until a year ago."

"Now I remember. Sometimes Andy came to High Hills to haul horses. Mostly he worked at Klaus's other farm, so I didn't really know him."

"His other farm?" Nancy queried.

"Klaus has a farm in Iowa, right across the state line," Lee Anne explained. "He keeps his brood-mares there. Aristocrat stays there in the spring during breeding season. Recently Klaus said something about getting a new stallion. I've never been to the Iowa farm because it has no riding facilities, but Michael goes there sometimes to work with yearlings."

"Thanks, Lee Anne." Nancy yawned and started to undress. The lack of sleep was catching up with her.

"Was that helpful?" Lee Anne slid back under the covers.

"I hope so. Now go back to sleep." As she pulled off her jeans, Nancy thought about everything she'd learned. Brackett must have worked with Aristocrat in Iowa, so he'd have to know how valuable the stallion was. And he might have known Michael, too.

Nancy frowned. That meant the two could have planned the theft together, and when Gilly found out what they'd done . . .

Nancy shivered, trying not to think about the groom. She glanced down at Lee Anne. Her eyes were closed, and she was breathing deeply. Nancy definitely didn't want to tell her friend the latest news, since it didn't help to clear Michael.

"Boy, I feel better." Nancy stretched. It was eight-thirty Sunday morning. Bess was already awake and dressed in shorts and a T-shirt.

"You look nice," Nancy said. "Going somewhere special?"

"Gunter's riding later this morning. He invited me to come watch—and help." She held up one foot. "That's why I'm wearing sneakers instead of sandals."

Nancy smiled. "Delicate sandals aren't too useful around horses. So you'll be with him most of the day?"

"Yes, but maybe all four of us can meet somewhere for lunch."

"I think Ned and I are going to tour a farm in Iowa." She filled Bess in on all they'd discovered.

Bess looked sad. "I hope, for Lee Anne's sake, you find out Michael and this Brackett guy had nothing to do with each other."

"Me, too." Nancy glanced around the room. "Where is Lee Anne?"

"She left early. She had to feed the horses, and she's grooming and exercising Curio. She still insists that Michael's innocent and will be out of jail in time for his test tomorrow, so she wants Curio to be ready."

Looking in the mirror, Bess checked her hair, then picked up her purse. "See you later."

"Have a good time," Nancy said. Reaching for the phone, she dialed the hospital. There was no change in Gilly's condition. Then she phoned Ned's room. His voice was thick with sleep. "Rise and shine, Detective Nickerson," she said. "We have criminals to apprehend."

Half an hour later they were driving to the showgrounds. "We'll stop at the barn first and ask Klaus about Brackett," Nancy said as she drove into the parking lot. She and Ned had grabbed a couple of bagels from the buffet at the motel before heading on their way. "But let me do the talking."

"That's okay with me." The window was down, and the rushing air ruffled Ned's brown hair. Nancy had dragged him out before he was quite ready, and he still looked half asleep.

They stopped at the security booth to show their passes, then drove into the parking lot beside Barn C.

"Good," Nancy said. "Klaus's Mercedes is here. He might have some news about Michael."

They found Klaus in the barn, chewing out a young groom who held a bucketful of cleaning supplies. Nancy hadn't seen the girl before and wondered if she'd been recruited to help Lee Anne.

When he saw Nancy and Ned, Klaus dismissed the girl with a curt "Be quick," then turned to greet them.

"Miss Drew, Mr. Nickerson, what brings you to the barn this morning?" he asked in his formal manner.

"We've been looking into the theft of Aristocrat," Nancy said.

Raising his hands and lifting his chin, Klaus looked skyward as if imploring the heavens. "My poor horse. And now Michael. My head is splitting with all the pain."

And what about Gilly? Nancy wanted to add, but instead she said, "You mentioned that you thought the guards might have stolen Aristocrat. Did you recognize any of them? Perhaps one of them might have been out to High Hills."

"Hmm." Klaus wrinkled his forehead as if pondering the question.

Nancy had purposely refrained from mentioning Andy Brackett's name. She wanted Klaus to identify the man on his own.

"No, I can't say I recognized anyone."

Nancy was surprised by his response. Andy Brackett might be nondescript, but if he'd worked for Klaus, Klaus should have recognized him.

"I spoke with Michael this morning," Klaus said, making a clicking noise of disgust. "My lawyer should have him out in no time—insufficient evidence. Those thickheaded police never should have arrested him in the first place."

Nancy studied the trainer's face. "You seem certain that Michael is innocent."

"I know the boy like a son," Klaus said. "Besides, why would he attack Gilly? There is no motive, as you Americans say in your detective shows."

Nancy lowered her voice. "Perhaps there was a motive. Gilly might have caught Michael stealing Aristocrat."

Klaus's chin snapped up. "That is absurd."

"Not totally. You see, Mr. Schaudt, we discovered that one of the guards used to work for you, and Michael knew him. They might have planned the theft together. Perhaps they attacked Gilly when she stumbled onto their scheme."

Brows arched, Klaus assessed Nancy with his direct gaze.

She didn't blink.

"That's an interesting theory, Miss Drew. However, if Michael needed money, he didn't have to steal a horse. All he had to do was ask me for a loan. And Andy Brackett is too dense to plan a theft. Still, I will definitely mention his name to Mr. Texel."

"In the meantime," Ned chimed in, "Nancy and I are going to your—"

Letting out a shout, Nancy shoved Ned hard. "Look out!"

The blow caught Ned by surprise. He stumbled backward, falling in a pile of manure. "What in the world—" he sputtered.

Quickly Nancy crouched beside him. "I am *so* sorry!" she apologized loudly, cutting him off. "But a wasp was buzzing around your head, and you know how allergic you are to wasps."

"Oh, right," Ned said quickly. "My allergies." He glanced up at Klaus, who must have thought they'd both gone mad. "Thanks for saving me from the killer wasp, Nan."

Nancy bit her lip to keep from laughing. Holding out her hand, she helped him up. The seat of his shorts was covered with manure.

"Oh, yuck. We'd better go back to the motel so you can change." Nancy turned toward Klaus. "Thanks for the information. Make sure you tell Texel about Brackett and keep us posted on Michael."

Grabbing Ned's elbow, she hurried him out of the barn.

"Couldn't you have thought of some other way to get my attention?" Ned complained playfully when they got outside.

"I'm sorry I pushed you, but I didn't want Klaus to know we were going to his farm. Did you hear what he said?"

Ned nodded. "When you asked Klaus whether he recognized any of the guards, he said no. Then two sentences later he mentioned that Andy Brackett is too dense to plan a theft."

Nancy stopped by the door of the Mustang. "Right! Only I never said Andy's name. Which means that Klaus knows Andy *and* knows he's working here." Pulling her keys from her purse, she unlocked the door.

"Why do you think he did that?" Ned asked.

"Good question." Nancy paused before opening the door. "Maybe Klaus knew he was working here all the time because he'd arranged it."

Suddenly Nancy's mind whirled back to the horse theft. She and Gilly had been sitting on the tack trunk. Gilly had been about to tell her something when they heard footsteps. Nancy clearly remembered the horror-struck expression on Gilly's face when she saw that it was Klaus.

"Ned, I think I've figured out what Gilly was going to tell me," Nancy exclaimed. "That Klaus Schaudt arranged the theft of his own horse!"

# *12*

## *Puzzling Clues*

"But why would Schaudt steal his own horse?"
Ned asked.

Nancy shook her head as she got into the
driver's side of the Mustang. "I'm not sure.
Perhaps Aristocrat's insured against theft and
Klaus hopes to collect on it." She pulled a towel
from the floor of the backseat and draped it over
the passenger seat. "Here. Sit on this." Climbing
in, Ned lowered himself gingerly onto the towel.

"After you change, then we'll go to Schaudt's
Iowa farm." Nancy started the car. "I'd love to
get a look at his files. If we can connect him to
Brackett and find a reason for him to steal his
own horse, we just might crack this case."

They stopped at a fast-food restaurant on the

way to the motel and got a take-out order. Even though it wasn't quite lunchtime, the two were hungry after their quick breakfast. When they got to the motel, Nancy waited outside while Ned ran in and changed.

"You look better," she told Ned ten minutes later when he climbed into the Mustang wearing clean jeans.

"Definitely an improvement," Ned said, strapping on his seat belt as Nancy roared off. She'd gotten directions to Klaus's other farm from Lee Anne. It was about a half hour's drive.

Reaching behind him, Ned pulled the two paper bags from the backseat and handed one to Nancy. "Now for those burgers."

Driving in silence, they concentrated on eating their lunch. The Illinois countryside was picturesque. Even though her mind was whirling with thoughts about the case, Nancy was able to relax—for the first time since she'd arrived at the horse park, she realized.

They took the first exit off the highway after crossing the state line into Iowa, then headed west on a winding road. The farm was just beyond the second left turn.

"Wow." Ned whistled when Nancy steered the Mustang along the gravel drive. "Nice digs."

White four-board fences ran parallel to the drive, enclosing lush pastures on both sides. In the field on their right, a dozen mares with foals grazed. On their left, a small band of yearlings romped.

When they topped a low hill, Nancy braked and let the car idle as she surveyed the farm below. The fencing ended at a large, very modern barn surrounded by trees. No cars or trucks were visible.

"Doesn't look as if anyone's here," Nancy said.

"Good. I didn't want to have to explain myself to some farmhand."

Nancy drove down the hill. Even though no vehicles were around, a caretaker could be on the premises. "If we do meet someone, we'll say we met Klaus at the show and he sent us to see his yearlings. That way, we'll at least get a tour of the place."

Ned chuckled. "Like we have the money to buy a horse."

Nancy parked. As soon as she switched off the engine, she heard dogs barking from somewhere around back.

Ned furrowed his brow. "They sound big and mean."

"Let's hope they're penned," Nancy said. She opened the car door, then waited. No dogs came barreling around the barn. "I think we may be okay."

Cautiously Ned opened his own door and climbed out. When he shut it, it made a sound as loud as a shotgun blast. "If that doesn't bring someone—or some critter—running, then there's probably no one here."

"We'd better hurry, though, before someone does show up." Nancy headed toward the barn. A set of double doors opened onto a wide aisle. She stepped inside. It was cool and dark out of the sun. Stalls flanked the aisle. As Nancy walked past them, she noted the brass name tag over each stall door.

"All of the horses must be outside," Nancy said as she looked into an empty stall. Then she heard a nicker and the thud of a hoof banging a wooden wall. *"Almost* all," she corrected.

The two hurried down the aisle. Nancy stopped in front of a closed wire-mesh stall door. The name tag read Salut.

"This must be Klaus's other stallion," Nancy guessed. The horse moved in front of the door and pressed his nose against the screen. "Hi, big guy," she crooned as she studied him.

Nancy frowned and moved closer. "Wow. This horse could be a ringer for Aristocrat. He's the same color, with no white markings."

"That's interesting," Ned said. "How do we know he's not Aristocrat?" Ned asked.

"We don't know," Nancy said. "But I know how to find out. Before she was hurt, Gilly told me to look for the scar on Aristocrat's hock. Remember? That's the way to identify him."

She unlatched the stall door. "This stallion is

wearing a halter. If you hold him, I'll check his hind leg."

"I hope he doesn't bite." Ned followed her into the stall. The big horse snorted suspiciously, but stood quietly while Ned held the cheekpiece of his halter.

"Easy, guy," Nancy soothed. Talking quietly, she moved around to the stallion's flank. Gilly hadn't said which hock, so she needed to check both.

Putting her left hand on his right flank, Nancy rubbed him to let him know she was there. He was such a powerful horse that one kick would have sent her flying.

"Just looking to see if you have a scar," she told him. Reaching down, she felt the joint in the hind leg. She probed the smooth hair gently until her fingers found a rough, jagged spot running along the inside of the leg.

"Ned!" Nancy whispered excitedly. "I found the scar Gilly was talking about!"

"Are you sure?"

"Yes. So that means either this is Aristocrat or Salut is his twin in every way."

"And if this is Aristocrat, then your hunch was right—Klaus stole his own horse," Ned said grimly.

"But why would he steal his own horse and then house him in his barn?" Turning, Nancy gave the horse a solid pat on his neck.

"Someone other than Gilly could have figured out that this is Aristocrat." As the stallion nuzzled her fingers, she frowned in confusion. "Unless . . ." She thought a minute, trying to make sense of it all. "Unless the horse that was stolen *wasn't* Aristocrat. I remember Gilly telling me that she couldn't find his scar. Maybe when she bathed him, she suddenly realized that the horse at the show wasn't Aristocrat at all."

"Why would Klaus pass off another horse as Aristocrat, then steal it?" Ned asked.

Nancy gave the horse one more pat, then followed Ned from the stall.

"And if that is Aristocrat in there"—Ned jerked his thumb toward the horse—"then who and where is Salut?"

Nancy locked the stall door behind her. "There've got to be answers to all our questions somewhere."

"I'll bet Klaus Schaudt knows the answers," Ned said.

"I doubt that he'll volunteer any information," Nancy said. Hands on hips, she looked up and down the aisle. "We'll have to hunt for the answers ourselves. Let's try searching the office."

"That must be it." Grabbing Nancy's hand, Ned led her down the aisle to a closed door. "Let's hope it's not locked." Ned turned the knob, and the door opened.

Nancy stepped inside. A window illuminated

the small paneled room. It was furnished with a wooden desk, a swivel chair, shelves, and a file cabinet. Paintings of horses decorated the walls.

"What are we looking for?" Ned asked.

"Any evidence that Andy Brackett worked here and insurance forms on Aristocrat." Sitting down in the swivel chair Nancy started opening the desk drawers while Ned headed for the file cabinet.

For ten minutes they worked in silence. Nancy searched through every drawer in the desk, locating stacks of new bills, correspondence from horse owners, and show schedules. Nothing had Brackett's name on it.

"Hey, the stuff in this file drawer might be helpful," Ned said. "Klaus has a folder on every horse."

Nancy popped out of the desk chair. "Let's see the one on Aristocrat."

Pulling out a folder, Ned held it up. "There's also one on Salut."

Quickly they scanned the two folders.

"Here are Aristocrat's registration papers," Nancy said. "They state his color, breed, sire, and dam."

"And here are Salut's." Ned took out a piece of paper and held it next to the one Nancy was holding. "They have the same parents. No wonder they look like twins. The only difference is that Salut is two years younger."

"How could they possibly have the same scar?" Nancy wondered. She pulled out several stapled papers. "Hey, here's Aristocrat's insurance policy. He's insured for one hundred thousand dollars." She frowned. "That's odd. Lee Anne said he was worth about two hundred thousand."

"Then he's worth more than his insurance would pay off if something happened to him," Ned pointed out.

Nancy heaved a sigh. "Which means all this knocks out my hunch that Klaus stole his own horse."

The sound of tires on gravel made the two teens start. "Someone's here!" Nancy gasped.

Hurriedly, they replaced the folders, then pushed the drawers and file cabinets shut. Nancy tiptoed to the door that opened into the barn and peered around the jamb. No one had come into the barn. "We can make a break out the far doors to our left, then run around to my car when the person comes inside."

"Whoever it is will still see your car," Ned whispered.

"I know, but we'll have to take a chance that we can get away before they see *us*." Gesturing to Ned, Nancy burst out of the office and raced for the open doors as loud barking erupted behind her.

Without slowing down, she tossed a glance

over her shoulder. Two burly rottweilers came galloping toward them, teeth bared.

Nancy felt her stomach churn as the dogs charged down the aisle after them, foam flying from their mouths. There was no way she and Ned would make it to the car in time!

# 13

## An Explanation

"This way, Nan!" Ned grabbed her hand, pulling her sharply to the right. She stumbled after him into an empty stall. Whirling, he slammed shut the wire mesh door.

Growling and snarling, the two dogs threw themselves at the door. Ned and Nancy had to brace their shoulders against it to keep the dogs from forcing it open. Nancy could feel the heat of their breath as their sharp teeth tore at the wire.

"Zeus! Apollo! Down!" a firm voice commanded.

Instantly the dogs backed off. Whining, they circled twice, then sat in the middle of the aisle. Nancy and Ned exchanged relieved glances. She didn't think they could have held the dogs off much longer.

Klaus Schaudt strode into view. He halted in front of the closed door and studied them. "Miss Drew, what are you and your friend doing in my barn?"

"Klaus, are we glad to see you!" Nancy greeted the trainer with forced cheerfulness. "Thank you for calling off your dogs. They scared us half to death."

That part was true, Nancy thought. She couldn't exactly say she was glad to see him. Nothing had confirmed her suspicions that Klaus and Andy Brackett were working together, but until she had some answers, she didn't trust the man.

"We were following the lead about the guard who worked for you," Nancy explained. "May we come out?"

"Of course. Zeus and Apollo were only doing their job. They are my farm's security. Usually I let them roam while I am gone. They definitely deter trespassers."

"Gee, I can't understand why," Ned muttered, eyeing the dogs as he opened the door and stepped into the aisle. Nancy followed right behind him. The rottweilers were still obeying the sit command, but she knew if Klaus gave the word, the dogs would be at their throats.

Klaus folded his arms. "You should have told me you planned to come to the farm, Miss Drew," he said. "I would have advised you not to bother. I informed Mr. Texel about Andy Brackett, but the man seems to have disappeared. I'd say that points to his possible guilt in the theft of Aristocrat."

"It does appear that way," Nancy agreed. "And since he worked for you, he must have known the stallion's value."

Klaus nodded. "He knew. And since he was a guard at the horse park he was in the perfect position to steal him. I thank you for discovering that fact. I wish I had identified him earlier." He folded his arms over his chest. "Of course, Mr. Texel wasn't aware of the connection, and I'm still not certain that he or one of his other men isn't involved. It would have taken at least two people to pull off the theft."

"That's exactly what I thought," Nancy said. "Someone had to drive the van or trailer that hauled Aristocrat away."

"And Michael Raines was *not* one of the thieves," Klaus stated firmly.

"We don't know that for sure," Ned said. "We saw your stallion Salut. He sure looks like Aristocrat."

"He should. They are brothers. When Aristocrat was so successful, I bought Salut, importing him from Germany this spring." Klaus's chin dropped to his chest. "It's a good thing, since we may never find my Aristocrat."

His sadness was so real that Nancy suddenly doubted he could have been in on the horse theft. Still, she had to ask him some questions. "Did you have an insurance policy on Aristocrat?" she asked. She already knew the answer, but she wanted to hear what Klaus would say.

"Yes. Though it will never cover his present or future worth. Anyway, money cannot replace a friend."

Klaus's words confirmed what Nancy and Ned had discovered. Obviously, he had no motive to steal the horse. She remembered Gilly's reaction when Klaus came into the stall after the theft. And what about the scar? Nancy thought.

"Gilly told me that Aristocrat had a scar on his hock," she continued, watching him closely. "It's odd that Saluut has one, too."

Anger flared in Klaus's eyes. "You went into his stall without my being here?"

Nancy held his piercing gaze. "You asked me to investigate, so I did."

Klaus inhaled slowly, his face reddening. Nancy knew he was used to being obeyed, not challenged.

"That I did," he admitted, but his tone was cool. "And Salut has no scar. He scraped his hock several days ago playing in his paddock. The hair has not had a chance to grow back in."

121

Nancy was satisfied with Klaus's explanations. In fact, everything he said made sense. "Thank you for answering my questions. We're sorry we came on your property without telling you. We'll head back to the horse park to find out if Texel or the police have located Andy Brackett."

"That sounds like a good plan." Klaus made a clicking sound, and immediately the dogs stood at attention and watched him, waiting for their next signal. "I wish I had something more to tell you about Mr. Brackett, but he left this farm a year ago."

"Was he fired?" Ned asked. "That might be another reason why he chose to steal your horse."

"Yes, I dismissed him for laziness."

Nancy could believe that. She bet Klaus expected his employees to jump the instant he spoke.

Nancy and Ned said goodbye. When they headed toward the doorway at the end of the aisle, Ned gave the rottweilers a wide berth.

Nancy didn't think Klaus would sic the dogs on them—though, on second thought, he'd gotten quite angry when he heard they'd been in Salut's stall.

Linking her arm through Ned's, she pulled him from the barn. "That was a close call," she said when they got outside.

"Do you think Klaus suspected we'd been in his office?" Ned asked.

"Let's hope not. He'd be furious, and I definitely don't want a second encounter with Jaws One and Two."

When they rounded the corner of the barn, Nancy paused to get her bearings. The bright sun was blinding. They were on the opposite side from where they had entered and had to jog back around the building to the Mustang.

After pulling open the door, Nancy scrambled into the seat and shut it firmly. Only when Ned was safe in the car did she let out a sigh.

"I love dogs, but those two gave me chills," she said as she pulled the keys from her jeans pocket and started the car.

"Me, too. Where to now? The horse park?"

"Yes. Let's hope Texel has found Andy Brackett. I want to call the hospital, too. If Gilly's conscious, she may be able to tell us who knocked her out. That would sure help us solve this case." She backed up, turned the Mustang, and headed up the drive.

"So you've crossed Klaus off your list of suspects?" Ned asked.

"He answered most of our questions," Nancy said. "Still—" She suddenly braked. Craning her neck, she leaned forward and looked out the windshield at a thick grove of trees and brush on the far side of the mare and foal pasture. In the middle of the grove, Nancy thought she'd spotted something solid and gray.

"What are you looking at?" Ned asked.

"There's something in those trees."

Ned looked out the window. "I see it. It looks like a metal shed."

"Or maybe a horse trailer?" Nancy checked the rearview mirror. They had crested the hill and were almost to the road, so the barn was behind them, out of sight. "Let's check it out."

Nancy drove out to the main road, turned left, and pulled onto the shoulder. She didn't know for sure what was in the trees. Still, the thing looked as if it had been hidden, concealed for a purpose, and that made Nancy suspicious.

"What if Klaus drives out?" Ned glanced over his shoulder.

"If he's headed back to the horse park, he'll take a right," Nancy said, opening her car door. "He won't see us."

"Unless he catches us running through his horse pasture," Ned said gravely.

Nancy punched him playfully on the shoulder. "Then we'll just have to run fast."

After locking the Mustang, she put the keys in her pocket. Then Nancy climbed the fence and, after checking to make sure no one was coming down the drive, jumped into the pasture. At the same time Ned jumped beside her, and the two of them tore across the field.

Nancy ducked between two saplings and into the brush, snagging her T-shirt on brambles. The grove was wilder and thicker than she'd thought.

"If only I hadn't left my trusty machete in the car," Ned joked as he pushed through the briars.

Holding her bare arms high, Nancy followed him. She was glad she'd worn long jeans. Halfway through the tangle of honeysuckle and cedars, she spied the gray thing about fifteen feet ahead of her. It was large and metal, like an old shed. When she moved closer, she knew her hunch was right—it was a horse trailer.

She caught her breath. "Ned, I think it's the trailer from the horse park!"

"Let's see if there's a dent." Whacking aside a branch, Ned made his way to the trailer. Someone had laid cedar branches against the side as if trying to camouflage the vehicle.

Ned knocked several branches to the ground. "There's the dent." He pointed to the side over the wheel. "It has to be the same trailer. But what is it doing here?"

"Good question." Nancy opened the side door, half expecting the grotesque mask to come flying out at her, but the trailer was dark and empty.

She sniffed. "Smells like horse manure."

"Gee, that's a big surprise." Ned laughed.

Nancy stepped into the trailer. The net, stuffed with what looked like fresh hay, still hung from the middle post. Had the trailer been used to haul Aristocrat away on the night he was stolen? she wondered.

"Nothing in there," Nancy said as she ducked back out. "But the fact that it's hidden makes it suspicious. We need to get the police to check it out." She stopped talking, suddenly realizing that Ned wasn't there. She looked right, then left. "Ned?"

"Around here!" he hollered from the far side of the trailer. Nancy hurried around the hitch to find Ned crouched, studying the ground.

"Tire tracks," he said as he stood up. "And they're fresh. This trailer hasn't been here long."

Nancy followed the tracks. The briars, broom grass, and honeysuckle were trampled in a wide path that stretched to the edge of the grove and came out in the pasture by the far fence.

"A pretty good hiding place," Nancy said, walking back to the trailer. "And I can think of only one reason someone would want to hide this trailer in here."

"So Klaus fooled us. He *was* in on the theft," Ned said in a low voice.

Just then Nancy heard a menacing growl behind her. The hair stood up on the back of her neck. Ned tensed and his eyes widened as he looked at something behind Nancy. "Don't move," he whispered.

"Good advice, Mr. Nickerson."

Slowly Nancy turned her head to look over her shoulder. Klaus stood on the path about eight feet behind her. Beside him, Andy Brackett, still dressed in his security uniform, a gun in a holster on his hip, held the two rottweilers on short leashes.

"It was you who stole Aristocrat," she said accusingly. "You and Brackett *were* in it together."

"So you figured it out," Klaus said smoothly. "I thought I had you convinced that it was all the doing of the hapless Mr. Brackett." He jerked his head toward Andy. "But I guess I didn't. Too bad, Miss Drew," he continued, his voice so cold it gave Nancy shivers. "I liked you. Now I'm afraid you and your friend will have an unfortunate accident like poor Gilly. Only this time we won't make a mistake."

# 14

## Seeing Double

"You were the one who hurt Gilly!" Nancy exclaimed as she spun to face Klaus. "Why? Did she figure out you stole your own horse?"

Klaus made a disdainful noise in his throat. "I can tell you haven't quite figured out my brilliant scheme yet, Miss Drew, and that makes me feel disappointed. I thought you were a worthy opponent."

"Nancy discovered your trailer," Ned said, his eyes on the dogs. They were straining against the leash. "You should have hidden it better."

"That was Brackett's stupidity." Klaus spat the last word. "If I'd been able to pull off the heist without an accomplice, I never would have trusted such an incompetent person."

Nancy threw Brackett a quick glance to see how he was taking Klaus's insults. The guard's face reddened, but he didn't say a word.

Her gaze shifted back to Klaus as she pondered the statement he had just made. What did he mean when he said she hadn't yet figured out his brilliant scheme?

"At least Brackett didn't bungle the fire and attempted theft of the other horse," Klaus continued. "They were nice distractions, don't you agree? They had Texel and his guards running every which way."

"Why did you frame Michael for Gilly's assault? How could you do that to someone you claim is like a son?" Nancy asked.

Klaus snorted. "The charges against Michael will never stick, though the frame-up went perfectly, except for *you*, Miss Drew. It was our misfortune that you scared Brackett away before he could silence Gilly for good."

"So you were the shadow I saw sneaking off," Nancy said to the guard.

Klaus arched an eyebrow. "He was. I was the person who drove the station wagon from the parking lot. Brackett ran from the barn, signaled to me, then hid."

"You had Michael's pass?" Ned asked.

"Slipped it off his dresser. Piece of cake, as you kids say."

"Klaus, what are we going to do with these

two?" Andy Brackett finally spoke. His voice was squeaky and lacked confidence. He wasn't the mastermind behind the theft, Nancy decided, but he must have been the perfect accomplice — easy to boss around.

"We'll take them back to the farm. Texel and the police already suspect you're the thief, Brackett. I'll say the two nosy teens discovered you trying to steal Salut, so you shot them, then ran off when I drove up."

"Sh-shot them?" Brackett stammered, raising his eyebrows. He opened his mouth as if to protest, but shut it quickly when Klaus spoke.

"You have a better idea?" the trainer snapped. "Don't worry, I'll give you enough money to leave the country. When this is over, I'll have lots of money."

He turned back to Ned and Nancy. "Now get moving." He nodded toward the tracks leading from the grove. "We've got to do this quickly. I will not allow two kids to ruin what took me years to plan."

Arms crossed, Nancy stood her ground a minute while her mind searched for a way out of the mess they were in. She and Ned couldn't just walk back to the farm. Once there, they'd be sitting ducks for whatever evil ending Klaus had in mind.

Narrowing his eyes, Klaus gave her a look of warning. "Do not doubt that Andy will turn the dogs on you at any time. He has trained them well. I can claim they were just doing their job when they found you trespassing on my property, but it would be a messy and painful way to go."

Nancy stifled a shudder. Linking his hand with hers, Ned tugged her gently toward the path. "Come on, Nancy. Let's do as he says."

Reluctantly, Nancy went with him. Klaus, Andy, and the two dogs followed right behind. They stepped into the pasture, startling the mares and foals, who quit grazing long enough to stare at them.

They walked down the hill toward the barn, Nancy's mind racing as she tried to figure out Klaus's scheme. He said the crime had taken him years to plan and he was going to make lots of money. Obviously, there was more to his scheme than the theft of one horse.

Since Klaus wouldn't receive that much insurance money from the loss of Aristocrat, he had to be making more money somehow. That was the puzzle. Unless . . .

Unless Aristocrat hadn't been stolen.

Gilly's hurried remark about not finding the scar on Aristocrat's hock stuck in Nancy's mind. If the horse at the park wasn't Aristocrat, then Klaus would get the insurance money—and he'd still have his horse. But what could he do with a horse that was supposed to have been stolen?

"Tell me, Klaus." Nancy slowed so she'd be

walking right in front of the trainer. "How long did it take you to find a ringer for Aristocrat?"

"So you are finally putting it together, are you?" Klaus replied, a touch of admiration in his voice. "I hoped to be able to share my brilliance with someone who would appreciate it."

"I know you're a smart man," Nancy said. "You wouldn't have planned something as risky as the theft of your own horse unless you could count on a big payoff. The insurance money obviously won't be enough."

They reached the fence in front of the barn. Stopping in the shade of a huge tree, Nancy faced him. "So you had another horse stolen, one that everybody thought was Aristocrat—everybody except Gilly."

"Yes, she figured it out, poor girl. She didn't even have to say anything. I knew it from the way she avoided me like a frightened rabbit."

"Then which horse was stolen?" Ned asked. He had climbed the fence and swung one leg over so he was straddling it. Below him, the dogs stared up hungrily.

"Tell them about the horse you stole, Brackett," Klaus said gruffly.

"Uh, I took that horse to an auction. The killers bought him."

"Killers!" Nancy exclaimed.

Klaus chuckled. "Yup. Right now he's being

hauled to a slaughterhouse, where they'll turn him into dog food."

"That's sick," Ned declared. "I thought you were a horse lover."

Klaus shrugged. "I had no ties to that horse. Andy discovered our Aristocrat look-alike in someone's backyard. It took a month to condition his coat and muscle him up so he'd be in the same shape as Aristocrat. We didn't bother to train him, since we planned to steal him before anyone rode him."

"Very clever," Nancy said, hoping to keep the man talking. "So where is the real Aristocrat? And what can you do with a horse that you're not supposed to have anymore?"

Throwing back his head, Klaus laughed heartily. "That's the best part, Miss Drew. Aristocrat is alive and well and will soon be making me lots of money. Only you'll have to figure that part out yourself, since we're running out of time." His smile faded. "No more delays. Get over the fence and into the barn."

Ned jumped down on the other side and waited while Nancy climbed over. Klaus took the dogs who had to crawl on their bellies to get under the low board.

This is our chance to get away, Nancy thought, casting her gaze around for a safe place. They could run to the office, barricade themselves in, and call the police, but the barn was fifty yards away—the dogs would be on them in a second, Nancy realized.

"Go inside the barn, Miss Drew," Klaus said, his words concise and menacing. "And don't try anything."

They crossed the grass and went into the end of the barn where they'd first entered. Behind them, Nancy could hear Andy talking to Klaus in a low voice, but she couldn't catch his words. She did hear the hesitation in his voice. Andy Brackett didn't have the guts to shoot them, she decided. Klaus would have to do it.

Which gave her an idea.

As they passed Salut's stall, the stallion pressed his nose against the wire door and nickered a greeting. "Hello, my handsome boy," Klaus crooned as if talking to a baby.

That was when Nancy knew for sure what had happened to Aristocrat. Gilly had been right.

She whirled to face Klaus. "Salut *is* Aristocrat! That scar on his hock isn't a new injury; it's the scar Gilly was talking about. You're passing Aristocrat off as a new horse."

"Quite right, Miss Drew." Stopping in front of Salut's stall, he waved an arm dramatically. "Meet my new stallion, the impressive Salut, who already is attracting so much attention that people are eager to breed their mares to him. He's going to make me a fortune."

Ned's mouth had dropped open. "But how can you pass him off as a new horse?"

"I have carefully built my excellent reputation, Mr. Nickerson. Believe me, not one person questioned the authenticity of the forged import papers and registration. I have even made up a glowing show career for the fictitious Salut."

"But why couldn't you do that with Aristocrat? Why pass him off as a new horse?" Nancy asked.

"Raising and training horses takes an incredible amount of money. I need that one hundred thousand dollar insurance money to build this farm up into a showplace that screams 'success and money.' I don't want to wait five years for my dream farm. I want it now."

"And you're willing to kill for it," Nancy said in a soft voice. The words were for Andy's benefit. She already knew Klaus would kill. Anyone who had no qualms about bumping off his employee and setting up someone he called his son would be capable of killing two people he didn't care about. If she was right, Andy Brackett might not be so heartless.

When she glanced surreptitiously at Brackett, she knew her hunch was right. He was shifting uncomfortably from foot to foot, his expression one of distress. It was then that Nancy realized the guard had purposely bungled Gilly's "death." He had never intended to kill the groom.

"I don't look at it as killing, Miss Drew," Klaus

stated. "I look at it as an investment in my future."

Nancy pointed to Andy. "What about *his* future? With two murders pinned on him, he will be hunted by the police forever."

"That's his problem," Klaus retorted. "He knew when he joined up with me that he'd be breaking the law."

"But *murder?*" Ned said dramatically, as if he knew what Nancy was trying to do.

Andy Brackett cleared his throat. "They're right, Klaus. Stealing a horse is one thing, but shooting—"

"Silence!" Klaus chopped the air with a hand. Instantly the dogs stood at attention, their black eyes trained on him. "You will obey, my stupid helper."

Brackett gulped, but he didn't back down. "This time I won't be silent, Schaudt. I only agreed to help you steal—"

"How dare you disobey!" Klaus roared angrily. Drawing back his arm, he punched the unsuspecting guard in the jaw. Nancy stifled a gasp as Andy staggered backward, hit the stall wall, and slumped to the floor, dazed.

Nancy raised her eyes to Klaus, whose face was red with fury.

"No one disobeys me," he thundered. Then an eerie grin spread slowly over his face. "Actually this is perfect. I can say I came into the barn just as Brackett shot you. To save my own life and apprehend the killer, I sent the dogs after him."

"You'll never get away with it," Ned said.

"And who's going to stop me, Mr. Nickerson? Texel and his clowns? Now, get in that stall or I'll give the dogs the signal to turn you into hamburger."

Nancy and Ned backed into the stall, Klaus moving with them. As he passed Andy's body, he snorted disdainfully. "The man will be better off dead anyway. He's such a mouse, he would have ruined everything." He chuckled and gave his stunned accomplice a kick.

Deep growls came from the throats of both dogs. Nancy froze, staring at the rottweilers in horror. The two dogs were glaring at Klaus with undisguised hatred.

Klaus didn't seem to notice. "Sit," he ordered, but the dogs ignored him. The hair rose on their backs. Their teeth gleamed in the dim light. Only then did the blood drain from Klaus's face as he finally realized the dogs were not going to obey him.

Beside her, Ned squeezed Nancy's shoulder. She looked at him, and he nodded toward the barn doors. She knew what he was signaling. While the dogs were distracted, she and Ned had to make a break for it. It was their only chance.

"Sit!" Klaus hollered again. He backed away from the dogs, his attention momentarily off the teens.

Grabbing Nancy's hand, Ned took off for the barn doors.

"Zeus! Apollo! Attack!" Klaus yelled, and an instant later the roar of the dogs followed by the trainer's hoarse scream filled the barn.

# 15

## Winners!

"Don't look back!" Ned warned as he and Nancy ran toward the Mustang. As they reached the car, the wail of sirens filled the air.

Glancing up the drive, Nancy saw two police cars and Texel's truck fly over the hill. With a gasp of relief, she sagged against the Mustang.

Ned ran toward the cars, waving his hands in the air. They screeched to a halt, and two Iowa State Highway Patrol officers jumped out.

"Inside the barn," Ned told them breathlessly. "The dogs have Klaus Schaudt, the owner of the farm. Schaudt's partner is in there, too. He's injured."

"Don't hurt the dogs!" Nancy cried. "They saved our lives."

The officers jogged into the barn just as Texel lumbered over. "What in tarnation is going on?" he thundered.

"Klaus was behind the theft of the horse," Nancy explained.

Texel didn't look surprised. "I never liked that pompous snob," he muttered as he headed for the barn doors.

"Only it wasn't Aristocrat that was stolen," Nancy continued, striding beside him. "They substituted a horse that looked just like him."

This stopped Texel in his tracks. "What?"

"It's a long story," Ned said. "When we figured out his scheme, Klaus decided to get rid of us—permanently."

Texel glowered. "That snake. Come on. I want to make sure my officers get them."

Ned and Nancy followed him into the barn. Andy Brackett was still slumped against the stall wall, holding a handkerchief to his bleeding lip. The dogs stood over him, licking his face and whining.

On the other side of the aisle, Klaus stood facing the wall, his head down. His shirt had been torn to shreds. One of the police officers was cuffing his hands.

When Klaus turned and saw Nancy and Ned, he barked, "That's them. They're the ones you should be arresting. They broke into my barn and tried to steal—"

"Save it for your lawyer, Schaudt," Texel snapped. "Because you're going to need one. Your groom already pointed the finger at you."

"Gilly's conscious?" Nancy asked excitedly.

"Yup. She told us that when she discovered the horse at the show wasn't Aristocrat, she knew right away that Schaudt had to be involved. Then Lee Anne mentioned that you'd asked her for directions to Schaudt's farm. That's why we were able to arrive just in time."

"How did Gilly figure out that Klaus was the thief?" Ned wondered.

"She knew that the only thing the guy loves besides money and himself is that horse," Texel explained. "So she figured there was no way anyone could have switched animals without him knowing."

"Bah," Klaus spat. "The blow on Gilly's head addled her brain. I'm telling you it was Brackett all along. He was in it with these two juvenile delinquents, so don't believe a word any of them say."

Texel only shook his head. "Klaus, you've been giving orders for so long, it's hard for you to believe that, for once, no one's going to jump when you bark. Especially since Gilly said she saw you the night she got whacked on the head."

Klaus's face turned white. "Nonsense!" he sputtered. "It was Brackett. He knew about the rasp in Michael's trunk. He sneaked into the stall and hit Gilly before she even saw him."

"Brackett may have whacked her, but she *did* see you. Before she lost consciousness, she spotted you smirking outside the stall." Texel jerked his head to the two officers. "Get him out of here, and then come get Brackett. Take them to the county police station. I'll be there in a minute, and we'll see how many charges Iowa and Illinois can pin on them."

Flanking Klaus, the two officers led him out of the barn. Nancy could hear his bellowing protests the whole way.

"What will happen to Andy Brackett?" Ned asked. The guard was still slumped on the floor, the two dogs lying by his side.

"He did try to save our lives," Nancy pointed out.

"We'll see how willing he is to talk," Texel said. "If Brackett gives us enough information to nail Klaus as the mastermind, maybe the police will go easy on him. Personally I want to see the greedy Herr Schaudt go to jail for a long time."

"Me, too," Nancy said.

"Curio has never looked better," Nancy told Lee Anne Monday morning. The two were sitting on the hillside, watching Michael and Curio perform a fabulous test. "You did a great job of keeping him in shape for Michael."

"Thanks," Lee Anne said, but her attention was on Michael and Curio. The duo had completed a high-stepping trot in place. Bursts of enthusiastic clapping from the audience had accompanied each movement the horse performed, so Nancy figured the pair must be doing well.

Nancy had to give Michael some credit. Yesterday afternoon, when he got out of jail, his mind had been focused on only one thing—riding this test. Nancy hadn't liked the way he ignored everything and everybody, but she finally understood that it was the only way he was able to emerge a winner.

Glancing to her left, she scanned the crowd. Bess and Ned had gone to pick up Gilly from the hospital while Nancy helped Michael and Lee Anne with the horses. Even though the doctors had told Gilly to go home to rest, the groom had insisted on coming to the event.

Nancy saw Ned, Bess, and Gilly on the opposite side of the arena. Gunter had joined the trio as they watched the last minutes of Michael's test. When Gilly spotted Nancy, she waved excitedly. Except for the white bandage wrapped on her head, the groom looked great.

Michael trotted Curio into the center of the arena, halted, and saluted the judge. With a roar of approval, the crowd stood and applauded him.

"That was the best test he's ever ridden!" Lee

Anne exclaimed, tears of happiness and pride filling her eyes. "I'm going down to join him."

She ran ahead. Nancy made her way through the horses, riders, and spectators until she found Gilly, Bess, Gunter, and Ned. "You look great!" she told Gilly.

"So did Michael," Gilly said. "I need to find him and congratulate him."

"And I need to apologize to him," Nancy murmured.

Putting an arm around her shoulders, Ned gave her a squeeze. "You didn't put Michael in jail, Nan. The evidence did."

The two went over to the edge of the crowd where Michael had halted Curio. When he dismounted, he was grinning.

"Perfect ride!" Lee Anne exclaimed when she ran up to him. Nancy half expected Michael to scoff at her. Instead, he wrapped his arms around her, pulled her close, and gave her a big kiss.

"Thanks to you," he said when he straightened up.

Lee Anne blushed bright red.

"One thing jail did for me was give me plenty of time to think," he told her. "I know I need to concentrate on my riding to win, but I also decided that riding isn't the only important thing in life."

"Good attitude," Gunter said. He offered Michael his hand. "Which makes for a good ride," he added.

Still grinning, Michael accepted the handshake and the compliment.

Nancy let out a sigh of relief. She was glad to see that Michael was human after all.

When Lee Anne went off with him and Curio, Nancy turned to Gilly. "Thank you for saving our lives. If you hadn't told Texel everything you knew, Ned and I would have been dog food."

Gilly squeezed Nancy's hand. "Thank you. If you hadn't come into the barn when you did, I think Klaus would have come into the stall and killed me." Her face grew pale. "I'll never forget the evil smirk on his face when I saw him outside the stall that morning. He looked possessed."

"He was," Ned said. "With greed."

Gunter shook his head. "It's so horrible to see what greed can do to a person. Herr Schaudt had a wonderful reputation. His ex-wife, Ruth, is still in Germany. She is one of the country's top trainers."

"Michael knows her," Gilly said. "He already called and told her what had happened. She's flying in tonight."

"I hope not to bail Klaus out," Bess sputtered angrily.

"No. To help keep the two farms running," Gilly explained. "Michael hopes she will take them over."

Gunter nodded. "She would be the one to do it. She will take good care of her horses and her employees."

"What's going to happen to Klaus?" Bess asked.

"We don't know yet." Just then Nancy spotted Texel lumbering across the showgrounds. "Texel might have an update."

"Good news!" he called as he approached the teens. "Between Andy Brackett's testimony and Gilly's, we should have enough to put Klaus away for a good long time."

Nancy grinned. Ned punched the air with his fist. "*Yes!*"

"Andy will be charged with assault," Texel went on. "But that's nothing compared to attempted murder."

"So everything's wrapped up," Nancy said. She knew Klaus would probably hire a regiment of lawyers. Still, the evidence was pretty solid against him.

"Not everything." Ned frowned. "I can't get that other horse out of my mind."

"What other horse?" Bess asked.

"The one that was stolen," Ned told her. "The one that ended up going to the slaughterhouse."

Texel slapped him on the back. "Don't look so gloomy, son. Even that has a happy ending."

"It does?" Ned perked up, and Gilly looked interested, too.

"Seems Brackett couldn't bear to sell the horse to the killers so he gave it to a friend of his who lives in the boondocks where no one would ever find it," Texel explained. "He made up some story about its being an old broken-down show horse that the owner wanted to get rid of."

Gilly smiled. "Even though I only took care of him for a couple of days, I knew he was a nice horse. Does he have a good home now?"

"The best," Texel said. "I personally checked the place out this morning. After all, that horse is evidence. Lucky is doing well in a pasture full of grass with two little girls to love him."

"Lucky?" Ned laughed. "That's a perfect name. He was lucky to escape the auction."

"A perfect name is right," Texel agreed. "In fact, I'd say we were all lucky."

"Why is that?" Bess asked.

Texel grinned at Nancy. "We were lucky you happened to be at this show, Nancy Drew!"

# NANCY DREW® MYSTERY STORIES  By Carolyn Keene

A MINSTREL® BOOK

## Published by  Pocket Books

# THE HARDY BOYS® SERIES  By Franklin W. Dixon

**Do your younger brothers and sisters want to read books like yours?**

**Let them know there are books just for _them!_**

They can join Nancy Drew and her best friends as they collect clues and solve mysteries in

# THE NANCY DREW NOTEBOOKS®

Starting with

#1 The Slumber Party Secret

#2 The Lost Locket

#3 The Secret Santa

#4 Bad Day for Ballet

**AND**

**Meet up with suspense and mystery in Frank and Joe Hardy: The Clues Brothers™**

Starting with

#1 The Gross Ghost Mystery

#2 The Karate Clue

#3 First Day, Worst Day

#4 Jump Shot Detectives

Look for a brand-new story every other month at your local bookseller

A MINSTREL® BOOK

Published by Pocket Books                    1366-02

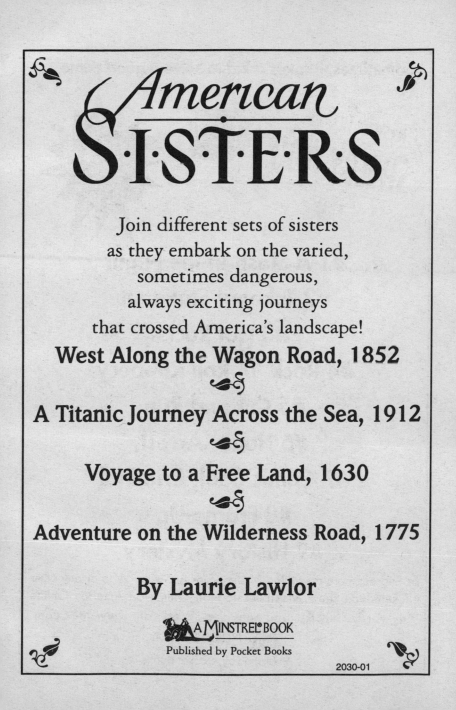

# American SISTERS

Join different sets of sisters
as they embark on the varied,
sometimes dangerous,
always exciting journeys
that crossed America's landscape!

## West Along the Wagon Road, 1852

## A Titanic Journey Across the Sea, 1912

## Voyage to a Free Land, 1630

## Adventure on the Wilderness Road, 1775

## By Laurie Lawlor

A MINSTREL BOOK

Published by Pocket Books

**Sometimes, it takes a kid to solve a good crime....**

Original stories based on the hit Nickelodeon show!

To find out more about *The Mystery Files of Shelby Woo* or any other Nickelodeon show, visit Nickelodeon Online on America Online (Keyword: NICK) and on the Web at www.nick.com.

A MINSTREL BOOK

Published by Pocket Books

1338-07